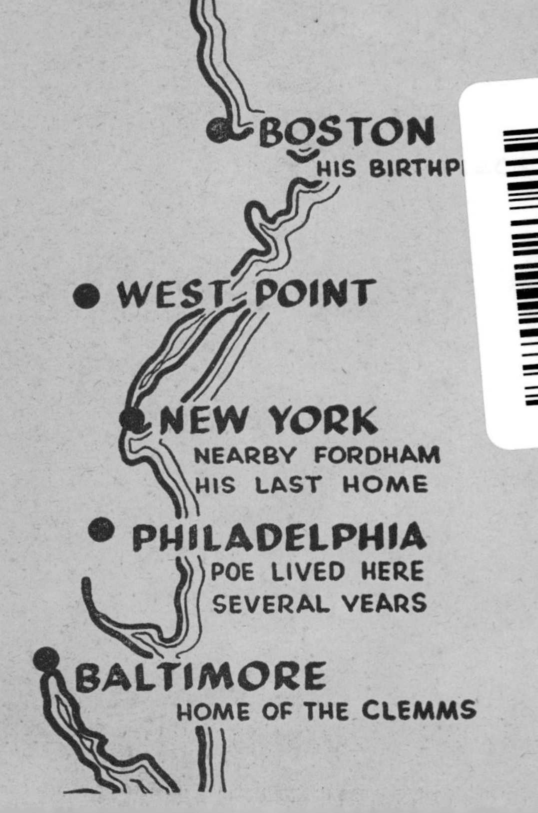
BOSTON
HIS BIRTHP
WEST POINT
NEW YORK
NEARBY FORDHAM
HIS LAST HOME
PHILADELPHIA
POE LIVED HERE
SEVERAL YEARS
BALTIMORE
HOME OF THE CLEMMS

D1453075

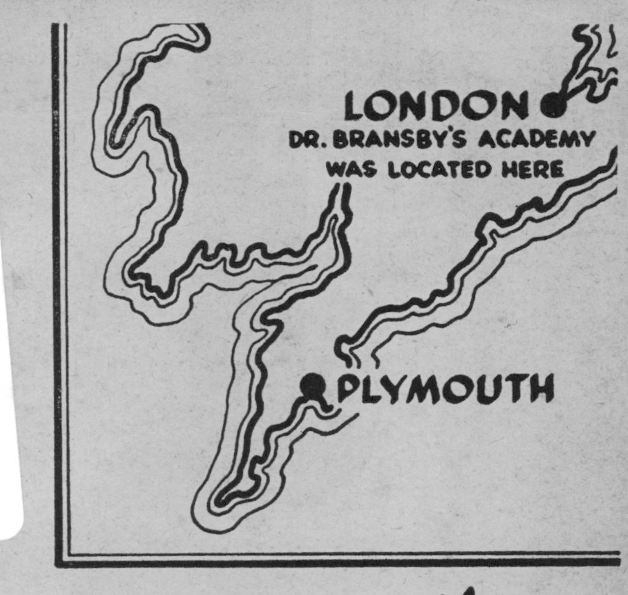
LONDON
DR. BRANSBY'S ACADEMY
WAS LOCATED HERE
PLYMOUTH
Ocean

# IN SUNSHINE AND SHADOW

*Pages from Poe*

*A gallant knight*
*In sunshine and in shadow,*
*Had journeyed long,*
*Singing a song,*
*In search of Eldorado.*

EDGAR ALLAN POE: *Eldorado*

EDGAR ALLAN POE

*CEBCO CLASSICS FOR ENJOYMENT*

# IN SUNSHINE AND SHADOW

## *Pages from Poe*

ADAPTED BY LOU P. BUNCE

HEAD OF THE ENGLISH DEPARTMENT, HIGHLAND PARK HIGH SCHOOL, HIGHLAND PARK, NEW JERSEY

EDITED BY MABEL DODGE HOLMES

HEAD OF THE ENGLISH DEPARTMENT, KENSINGTON HIGH SCHOOL, PHILADELPHIA, PA.

*College Entrance Book Company, New York*

COPYRIGHT, 1946
BY COLLEGE ENTRANCE BOOK COMPANY, INC.

TYPOGRAPHY BY ROBERT JOSEPHY
ILLUSTRATIONS BY MARC LEGIS
PRINTED IN THE UNITED STATES OF AMERICA

# CONTENTS

## TALES

# PREFACE

THERE is much in life today to distract the minds of young people and keep them constantly over-stimulated. The moving picture thrillers, the fast-moving radio programs, the murder mystery magazines, the scientific wonder stories—all of these offer a short and easy route to diversion and excitement. Is it any wonder, then, that high school pupils often find the literature they read in school "stuffy" and consider the classics slow-moving and dull?

Certainly it is not the aim of English teachers to bore their students; nor do they want them to miss the great literature of the world merely because it does not seem, on the surface, easy to read and exciting. The problem is to find something for them of real value as literature and of sufficient interest as reading matter. The tales of Edgar Allan Poe fulfil both requirements.

Like the "gallant knight" of his own poem, Poe journeyed long in search of his Eldorado, his land of gold. Most of the way lay in shadow, the gloom of which hangs over the tales he found to tell. But the darkness is shot through with gleams of sunshine, the more brilliant because rare. It is this infinite variety that gives the tales their fascination and makes them ageless. "In Sunshine and Shadow" contains a selection of the tales that seem best suited to young people of high school age.

This adaptation of the tales follows the original as closely as possible. In some places long philosophical discussions have been omitted entirely; in others, descriptions have been shortened. Throughout, the vocabulary has been simplified. It has been the adapter's aim to preserve the "atmosphere" of Poe and to alter only as much as was necessary to make his writing understandable to students who find reading difficult.

The author wishes to express her appreciation to Dr. Mabel Dodge Holmes, Head of the English Department, Kensington High School, Philadelphia, Pa., to Grace A. Benscoter, Department of English, Emerson High School, Gary, Indiana, and to Prof. Glenn M. Blair, Assistant Professor of Educational Psychology, University of Illinois, Urbana, Illinois, for their valuable suggestions and criticisms in the preparation of the manuscript. She is also grateful to the members of the 1945 12H English class of the Highland Park, New Jersey, High School, who listened to each tale as it was completed and furnished ideas for its improvement; and to Miss Rita Goldstein and Miss Mary E. Bunce for their aid and encouragement.

The author is indebted to the Poe Foundation, Richmond, Va., Central Publishing Company and Dementi Studio, Richmond, Va., the Hughes Company, Baltimore, Md., Historical Society of Pennsylvania, Philadelphia, Pa., and to the Curator, Bronx Society of Arts and Sciences, Bronx, New York, for granting permission to use the illustrations contained in the life story of Poe.

L.P.B.

*March, 1946*

# *The Master Mind at Work*

# THE GOLD BUG

MANY years ago I became friendly with a Mr. William Legrand. He was of a fine old family and had once been wealthy; but a series of misfortunes had reduced him to poverty. To avoid being humiliated among his friends, he left New Orleans, the city of his ancestors, and went to live at Sullivan's Island, near Charleston, South Carolina.

This island is a very odd one. It consists of little else than the sea sand and is about three miles long. At its widest point it is no more than a quarter of a mile across. It is separated from the mainland by a narrow creek, which runs through reeds and slime. There are no trees of any height to be seen. Near the western shore, where Fort Moultrie stands, and where there are a few summer cottages, may be found some palmetto trees; but the whole island, with the exception of this western point and the hard white sand of the beaches, is covered with a dense undergrowth of sweet myrtle, which often grows to a height of fifteen or twenty feet and forms a fragrant thicket.

In the depths of these thickets, not far from the eastern end of the island, Legrand had built himself a small cabin, in which he lived when I first, by mere accident, made his acquaintance. This soon grew into friendship, for there was much about him that I liked and respected. I found him clever and well educated, though gloomy and moody at times. He had many books with him, but rarely used them. His chief amusements were hunting and fishing, or walking along the beach and through myrtles in search of shells or specimens for his bug collection. On these trips he was usually accompanied by an old negro called Jupiter, who had been freed from slavery before the family fortune was lost, but refused to be parted from his young "Massa Will."

The winters on Sullivan's Island are seldom very severe, and in the fall a fire is rarely necessary. About the middle of October, 18–, there occurred, however, a day of unusual chilliness. I scrambled through the underbrush to the cabin of my friend, whom I had not visited for several weeks. At that time I was living in Charleston, nine miles from the island. Upon reaching the cabin, I knocked, as was my custom. Getting no reply, I looked for the key where I knew it was always hidden, unlocked the door, and went in. A fine fire was blazing on the hearth. It was a novelty, and a welcome one. I took off my overcoat, settled down in an armchair near the crackling logs, and waited patiently for the arrival of my hosts.

Soon after dark they arrived and gave me a most cordial welcome. Jupiter bustled about to prepare supper. Legrand was in one of his enthusiastic moods. He had found an unknown shell-fish, and, more than this, he had hunted down and secured with Jupiter's assistance a scarab, a kind of beetle, which he believed to be entirely new, but about which he wanted to have my opinion the next day.

"And why not to-night?" I asked, rubbing my hands over the blaze and wishing scarabs had never been heard of.

"If I had only known you were here!" said Legrand. "But it's so long since I saw you. How could I know you would pay me a visit this night of all others? As I was coming home, I met Lieutenant G— from the fort, and very foolishly I lent him the bug; so it will be impossible for you to see it until morning. Stay here to-night, and I will send Jup down for it at sunrise. It is the loveliest thing in creation!"

"What? Sunrise?"

"Nonsense! No—the bug. It is of a brilliant gold color, about the size of a large hickory-nut, with two jet black spots near one end of the back and another somewhat larger at the other. The antennae are . . ."

"They ain't no tin in him, Massa Will, I keep a tellin' you," here interrupted Jupiter; "de bug is a goole-bug, solid, ebery bit of him, inside and all, sep' his wing. Neber felt half so heavy a bug in all my life."

"Well, suppose it is, Jup," replied Legrand, somewhat more seriously, it seemed to me, than the case demanded. "Is that any reason for your letting the supper burn? The color"—here he turned to me—"is really almost enough to justify Jupiter's idea. You never saw a more brilliant metallic luster than that of the scales—but you can't judge of that until tomorrow. In the meantime I can give you some idea of its shape." Saying this, he seated himself at a small table on which were pen and ink, but no paper. He looked for some in a drawer, but found none.

"Never mind," said he at length; "this will do;" and he took from his pocket a scrap of what looked to me like very dirty paper and made upon it a rough drawing with the pen. While he did this, I kept my seat by the fire, for I was still chilly. When the drawing was finished, he handed it to me without getting up. As I took it, we heard a low growl, followed by a scratching at the door. Jupiter opened it, and a large Newfoundland dog belonging to Legrand rushed in and leaped upon my shoulders with joy, for I had made a fuss over him during one of my previous visits. When he had settled down, I looked at the paper and found myself greatly puzzled at what my friend had pictured.

"Well!" I said, after studying it for several minutes, "this *is* a strange scarab, I must confess; new to me; never saw anything like it before—unless it was a skull—

which it looks more like than anything else *I* have ever seen."

"A skull!" echoed Legrand. "Well—it has something of that appearance on paper, no doubt. The two upper black spots look like eyes, eh? And the longer one at the bottom like a mouth—and then the whole shape is oval."

"Perhaps so," said I; "but, Legrand, I fear you are no artist. I must wait until I see the beetle itself, if I am to form any idea of its personal appearance."

"Well, I don't know," said he, a little offended. "I draw pretty well. I *should* anyway—have had good teachers, and flatter myself that I'm not entirely a dunce."

"But, my dear fellow, you are joking then," said I. "This is a very passable *skull*, and your scarab must be the queerest one in the world if it resembles it. And where are the antennae you spoke of?"

"The antennae!" said Legrand, who seemed to be getting strangely excited about the whole thing. "I'm sure you must see the antennae. I made them as clear as they are on the bug itself, and I should think that would be sufficient."

"Well," I said, "perhaps you have. Still, I don't see them," and I handed him the paper without further remarks, not wishing to annoy him. I was much surprised at the turn affairs had taken. His bad temper puzzled me—and as for the drawing of the beetle, there were positively *no* antennae visible, and the whole thing *did* bear a very close resemblance to the ordinary pattern of a skull.

He took the paper peevishly and was about to crumple it and throw it on the fire, when a glance at the pattern on it seemed to fix his attention. In an instant his face grew violently red—in another, just as pale. For several minutes he continued to examine the drawing carefully. At length he arose, took a candle from the table, and proceeded to seat himself on a sea-chest in the farthest corner of the room. Here again he made an anxious examination of the paper, turning it in all directions. He said nothing, however, and his conduct greatly astonished me; yet I thought it wise not to irritate him with any comment. Presently he took a wallet from his coat pocket, placed the paper carefully in it, and deposited both in a writing-desk, which he locked. He grew more calm, but his original air of enthusiasm had quite disappeared. Yet he seemed not so much sulky as absent-minded. As the evening wore away, he became more and more sunk in thought, from which no joking of mine could arouse him. It had been my intention to spend the night at his cabin, as I had frequently done before; but, seeing my host in this mood, I thought it wise to leave. He did not urge me to stay, but as I left he shook my hand with even more than cordiality.

It was about a month after this (and during the interval I had seen nothing of Legrand) when I received a visit in Charleston from his man Jupiter. I had never seen the good old negro so down-hearted, and I feared that some serious disaster had happened to my friend.

"Well, Jup," said I, "what is the matter now? How is your master?"

"Why, to speak de troof, Massa, he not so well as mought be."

"Not well! I am truly sorry to hear it. What does he complain of?"

"Dar! Dat's it! He neber 'plain of nothin', but he berry sick for all dat."

"*Very* sick, Jupiter! Why didn't you say so at once? Is he in bed?"

"No, dat he ain't—dat's just whar de shoe pinch. My mind is got to be berry heavy 'bout poor Massa Will."

"Jupiter, I should like to understand what it is you are talking about. You say your master is sick. Hasn't he told you what ails him?"

"Why, Massa, 'taint worth while to git mad about it. Massa Will ain't say nothin' the matter with him. But what make him go about lookin' dis way, wid his haid down and his shoulders up and lookin' as white as a goose? And then he keeps a writin' all de time wid figgers on a slate—the queerest figgers I ever see. I'se gittin' to be skeered, I tell you. Hab to keep a mighty tight eye on him. 'Tother day he give me a slip 'fore sun-up and was gone de whole ob de blessed day."

"But can you form no idea, Jupiter, of what has caused this illness, or rather this change of conduct? Has anything happened since I saw you?"

"No, Massa, dey ain't been nothin' unpleasant *since* —'twas *'fore* den I'm feared—'twas de day you was dar."

"How? What do you mean?"

"Why, Massa, I mean de bug—dar now!"

"The what?"

"De bug. I'm very sartin' Massa Will bin bit somewhere 'bout de haid by dat goole-bug."

"And what cause have you, Jupiter, for such an idea?"

"Cause enough, Massa. I neber did see such a bug. He kick an' bite everything what cum near him. Massa Will cotch him fuss, but had for to let him go mighty quick, I tell you—den was de time he must ha' got bit. I didn't like de look ob de bug myself, nohow, so I wouldn't take hold ob him wid my finger, but I cotch him wid a piece ob paper dat I found. I rop him up in de paper, and I stuff a piece ob it in his mouth—dat de way."

"And you think, then, that your master was really bitten by the beetle, and that the bite made him sick?"

"I don't think noffin' 'bout it—I know it. What make him dream 'bout de goole so much if 'taint cause he bit by de goole-bug? I'se heered 'bout dem goole-bugs 'fore dis."

"But how do you know he dreams about gold?"

"How I know? Cause he talk 'bout it in his sleep; dat's how I know."

"Well, Jup, perhaps you are right. But how did you happen to pay me the honor of a visit to-day? Did you bring any message from Mr. Legrand?"

"No, Massa, I bring dis here note," and here Jupiter handed me a note which said,

*"My dear——: Why have I not seen you for such a long time? I hope you have not taken offense at me.*

*"Since I saw you I have had great cause for anxiety. I*

*have something to tell you, but scarcely know how to tell it or whether I should tell it at all.*

*"I have not been well for several days, and poor old Jup annoys me almost beyond endurance with his attention.*

*"I have made no addition to my collection since we met.*

*"If it is at all convenient for you, come over with Jupiter.* Do *come. I wish to see you* tonight, *on business of importance. I assure you that it is of the* highest *importance.*

*"Ever yours,*
*"William Legrand"*

There was something in the tone of this note which gave me great uneasiness. Its whole style differed from that of Legrand. What could he be dreaming of? What had excited him so? What "business of the highest importance" could he possibly have to transact? Jupiter's account of him promised nothing good. I had a dread that his misfortunes had at length unsettled the reason of my friend. Without a moment's hesitation, therefore, I prepared to accompany the Negro.

Upon reaching the wharf, I noticed a scythe and three spades, all apparently new, lying in the bottom of the boat we were to take.

"What is the meaning of all this, Jup?" I inquired.

"Massa Will insist upon my buyin' dem for him in de town, and de debbil's own lot of money I had to gib for dem."

"But what, in the name of all that is mysterious, is your Massa Will going to do with scythes and spades?"

"Dat's more dan I know, and debbil take me if I don't b'lieve 'tis more dan he knows, too. But it's all come ob de bug."

Getting no more satisfaction from Jupiter, whose only thought was of "de bug", I stepped into the boat and set sail. With a fair and strong breeze we soon ran into the little cove to the northward of Fort Moultrie, and a walk of about two miles brought us to the cabin. It was about three in the afternoon when we arrived. Legrand had been awaiting us eagerly and grasped my hand with nervous emphasis. His face was ghastly pale, and his deep-set eyes glared with an unnatural light. After some questions about his health, I asked him if he had yet obtained the scarab from Lieutenant G——.

"Oh, yes," he replied, blushing violently; "I got it back from him the next morning. Nothing would tempt me to part with that scarab. Do you know that Jupiter is quite right about it?"

"In what way?" I asked, with sad fears of his sanity.

"In supposing it to be a bug of *real* gold." He said this with an air of deep seriousness, and I felt greatly shocked.

"This bug is to make my fortune," he continued with a triumphant smile, "to give me back my family possessions. Is it any wonder that I prize it? Since Fortune has presented it to me, I have only to use it properly and I shall secure the gold of which it is the token. Jupiter, bring me that scarab."

"What! The bug, Massa? I'd druther not trubble dat bug. You mus' git him for your own self."

Hereupon Legrand arose with a grave and stately air and brought the beetle from a glass case in which it had been placed. It was a beautiful scarab, and of course a great prize from a scientific point of view. There were two round black spots near one extremity of the back and a long one near the other. The scales were hard and glossy and like polished gold. The weight of the insect was remarkable, and, taking all things into consideration, I could hardly blame Jupiter for his ideas about it, but did not know what to make of Legrand's agreement with him.

"I sent for you," he said in an expressive way when I had completed my examination of the beetle, "I sent for you so that you could give me advice and help in following out the ideas of fate and of the beetle."

"My dear Legrand," I cried, interrupting him, "you are certainly not well and had better be careful. You go to bed, and I will stay with you a few days until you get over this. You are feverish and—"

"Feel my pulse," said he.

I felt it and, to tell the truth, found not the slightest indication of fever.

"But you may be ill and still have no fever. Let me prescribe for you this once. In the first place, go to bed. In the next—"

"You are mistaken," he interrupted. "I am as well as I can be, excited as I am. If you really wish me well, you will help me."

"And how is this done?"

"Very easily. Jupiter and I are going on a trip into the hills on the mainland, and we shall need the aid of someone whom we can trust. You are the only one who can help. Whether we succeed or fail, my excitement will be relieved by the trip."

"I am anxious to oblige you in any way," I replied, "but do you mean to say that this infernal beetle has any connection with your trip into the hills?"

"It has."

"Then, Legrand, I cannot help you in any such foolish adventure."

"I am sorry—very sorry—for we shall have to try it by ourselves."

"Try it by yourselves! The man is surely mad. But wait—how long do you plan to be absent?"

"Probably all night. We shall start immediately and be back at all events by sunrise."

"And will you promise me, upon your honor, that, when this spell of yours is over and the bug business settled to your satisfaction, you will then return home to follow my advice as though I were your doctor?"

"Yes, I promise; and now let us be off, for we have no time to lose."

With a heavy heart I accompanied my friend. We started about four o'clock, Legrand, Jupiter, the dog, and I. Jupiter had with him the scythe and spades. His manner was patient and "dat darn bug" the only words which came from his lips during the journey. I had charge of a couple of dark lanterns, while Legrand carried only the scarab attached to a bit of cord, which he twirled to and fro as he went. I still thought my friend was losing his mind, but considered it best to humor him until I could do something about it. In the meantime I tried, though all in vain, to find out from him the purpose of the expedition. He seemed unwilling to talk, however, and to all my questions replied, "We shall see."

We crossed the creek in a rowboat, and, climbing the high banks on the shore of the mainland, proceeded northwest through a tract of wild and desolate country. Legrand led the way with decision, pausing only for a minute now and then to check with landmarks which he had apparently made himself at some time.

In this manner we traveled for about two hours, and the sun was just setting when we reached a region more dreary than any we had yet seen. It was a sort of tableland. Near the top of a densely-wooded hill, huge crags were scattered about, and deep ravines made the scene still more wild.

The natural platform to which we had climbed was overgrown with briers. Jupiter, by order of his master, cleared a way through them with the scythe and made a path to the foot of an enormously tall tulip tree, which stood on the level with some eight or ten oaks. It was, however, much more beautiful than all of them in the size of its leaves, the wide spread of its branches, and the general majesty of its appearance. When we had reached this tree, Legrand turned to Jupiter and asked him if he thought he could climb it. The old man seemed a little staggered by the question and for some moments made no reply. At length, when he had walked slowly around the trunk and examined it carefully, he said, "Yes, Massa, Jup climb any tree he ebber see in his life."

"Then up with you as soon as possible, for it will soon be too dark to see what we are doing."

"How far up mus' I go, Massa?" inquired Jupiter.

"Get up the main trunk first, and then I will tell you which way to go. Stop! Take this beetle with you."

"De bug, Massa Will! De goole-bug?" cried the Negro, drawing back in dismay. "What for mus' I tote de bug up de tree? Darned if I do!"

"If you are afraid, Jup, a great big Negro like you, to take hold of a harmless little dead beetle, why, you can carry it up by this string. But if you do not take it up with you in some way, I shall be forced to break your head with this shovel."

"What's de matter now, Massa?" said Jup, shamed into consent. "Why you always want to fuss wid de old nigger? Was only jokin', anyhow. *Me* feered ob de bug? What I keer 'bout dat bug?" Here he took hold of the extreme end of the string, and, holding the bug as far away from him as he could, prepared to climb the tree.

A young tulip tree has a very smooth trunk; but as it grows older, the bark becomes gnarled and uneven. So it was not really hard for Jupiter to climb. After one or two narrow escapes from falling, he at length wriggled himself into the first great fork and seemed to think he had gone as far as necessary. He was now sixty or seventy feet from the ground.

"Which way mus' I go now, Massa Will?" he asked.

"Keep going up the largest branch, the one on this side," said Legrand. The Negro obeyed him promptly and with little trouble, climbing higher and higher until we could get no glimpse of him through the thick foliage. Presently his voice was heard.

"How much furder is I got to go?"

"How high up are you?" asked Legrand.

"I can see de sky fru de top ob de tree," replied the Negro.

"Never mind the sky. Listen to what I say. Look down the trunk and count the limbs below you on this side. How many limbs have you passed?"

"I done pass five big limbs, Massa, on dis side."

"Then go up one more limb."

In a few minutes he called down that he had reached the seventh limb.

"Now, Jup," said Legrand, evidently much excited, "I want you to work your way out on that limb as far as you can. If you see anything strange, let me know."

By this time I was sure that my friend was insane. I became very anxious about getting him home. While I was considering what was the best thing to do, Jupiter's voice was again heard.

"I'm afeered to venture far on dis limb. It's daid pretty much all de way."

"Did you say it was a dead limb, Jupiter?" cried Legrand in a shaking voice.

"Yes, Massa, daid as a door nail for sartin."

"What in the name of heaven shall I do?" asked Legrand seemingly in great distress.

"Do!" said I, glad of a chance to speak up; "why, come home and go to bed. Come now, like a good fellow. It's getting late. Remember your promise."

"Jupiter," cried he, without paying the least bit of attention to me, "do you hear me?"

"Yes, Massa Will, hear you plain."

"Try the wood with your knife and see if you think it *very* rotten."

"Rotten, sure nuff," replied the Negro in a few minutes, "but not so rotten as mought be. Might venture out leetle way on de limb by myself, dat's true."

"By yourself! What do you mean?"

"Why, I mean de bug. 'Tis *berry* heavy bug. S'pose I drop him down, and den de limb won't break wid just de weight ob one nigger."

"You rascal!" cried Legrand, apparently much relieved. "What do you mean by telling me such nonsense as that? As sure as you let that beetle fall, I'll break your neck. Jupiter! Do you hear me?"

"Yes, Massa; needn't holler at de pore nigger."

"Now listen. If you will venture out on the limb as far as you think safe and not let go of the beetle, I'll make you a present of a silver dollar."

"I'se gwine, Massa Will, deed I is," replied the Negro very promptly. "I'se mos' out to de end now."

"*Out to the end!*" screamed Legrand. "Do you say you are out to the end of that limb?"

"I'll soon be to de end, Massa. Oh! Lor-gol-a mercy! What is dis here on de tree?"

"Well!" cried Legrand, highly delighted. "What is it?"

"Why, a skull! Somebody lef' his head up de tree and de crows gobble ebery bit ob de meat off."

"A skull, you say! How is it fastened to the limb? What holds it on?"

"Dare's a great big nail in de skull, dat fastens it on to de tree."

"Jupiter, do exactly as I tell you, do you hear?"

"Yes, Massa."

"Pay attention then. Find the left eye of the skull."

"Why, dar ain't no eye lef' at all!"

"Don't be stupid. Do you know your right hand from your left?"

"Yes, I knows dat. 'Tis my left hand what I chops wood with."

"To be sure. You are left-handed; and your left eye is on the same side as your left hand. Now I suppose you can find the left eye of the skull, or the place where the left eye has been. Have you found it?"

There was a long pause. At length the Negro asked, "Is de lef' eye ob de skull on de same side as de lef' hand ob de skull too? Cause de skull ain't got a bit ob hand at all. Never mind! I got de lef' eye now. What mus' I do wid it?"

"Let the beetle drop through it as far as the string will reach. But be careful not to let go your hold of the string."

"All dat's done, Massa Will. Mighty easy ting to put de bug fru de hole—look out for him dar below."

The beetle now came in sight and gleamed in the last rays of the setting sun. Legrand took the scythe and cleared with it a circular space three or four yards in diameter just beneath the insect, and then ordered Jupiter to let go the string and come down from the tree.

Driving a peg into the ground at the spot where the beetle fell, my friend now produced from his pocket a tape-measure. Fastening one end of this at that point of the trunk of the tree nearest the peg, he unrolled it until it reached the peg and from that point on for fifty feet farther, Jupiter meanwhile clearing away the brambles with the scythe. At this point he drove in a second peg, and around this as the center made a rude circle about four feet in diameter. Taking a spade himself and giving one to Jupiter and one to me, Legrand begged us to start digging as quickly as possible.

I take no special pleasure in such an occupation at any time, and would have been glad to get out of it, for the night was coming on, and I was already tired. I saw no way to escape, however, and was afraid of upsetting my poor friend by refusing. I had a feeling that he had taken seriously some of the numerous Southern superstitions about buried treasure. His finding the scarab and Jupiter's idea that it was "a bug of real gold" would have encouraged him in his idea. On the whole I was much upset and puzzled, but concluded I couldn't get out of the digging.

The lanterns having been lit, we all fell to work as

though we were doing something really sensible. We dug very steadily for two hours. All was quiet except for the yelpings of the dog, who took a great deal of interest in our proceedings. He became so noisy that we were afraid he would alarm someone, or rather Legrand was afraid of it. I should have been glad of any interruption which would have made it possible to get him home. The noise was at length silenced by Jupiter, who tied up the animal's mouth with one of his suspenders.

At the end of the two hours we had reached a depth of five feet, and yet there were no signs of any treasure. Legrand, much annoyed, wiped his brow and went on digging. We had excavated the entire circle of four feet in diameter, and now we enlarged the hole all around by two feet. Still nothing appeared. The gold-seeker, whom I sincerely pitied, at length climbed out of the pit with the bitterest disappointment, and proceeded slowly and reluctantly to put on his coat, which he had taken off at the start of his labors. In the meantime I made no remarks. Jupiter, at a signal from his master, began to gather up his tools. This done and the dog unmuzzled, we turned in silence toward home.

We had taken only a dozen steps in this direction, when, with a loud oath, Legrand strode up to Jupiter and seized him by the collar. The astonished Negro opened his eyes and mouth to the fullest extent, let the spades fall, and fell upon his knees.

"You scoundrel," said Legrand, "you black villain, answer me this minute. Which is your left eye?"

"Oh, my golly, Massa Will! Ain't dis my lef' eye for

sartin?" roared Jupiter, placing his hand on the right one, and holding it there as if in fear his master would try to gouge it out.

"I thought so! I knew it! Hurrah!" shouted Legrand, letting the Negro go and dancing about with joy, much to the astonishment of Jupiter, who, arising from his knees, looked from his master to me and then from me to his master.

"Come! We must go back," said the latter; "the game's not up yet." And he again led the way to the tulip tree.

"Jupiter," said he, when we had reached its foot, "come here. Was the skull nailed to the limb with the face outward or the face to the limb?"

"De face was out, Massa, so dat de crows could get at de eyes good, widout any trouble."

"Well, then, was it this eye or that through which you dropped the beetle?" Here Legrand touched each of Jupiter's eyes.

" 'Twas dis eye, Massa, de lef' eye, jis as you tell me." And here it was his right eye that the Negro indicated.

"That will do. We must try it again."

Here I began to see some method to my friend's madness. He moved the peg which marked the spot where the beetle had fallen to a spot about three inches farther west. Taking the tape-measure and measuring with the same method he had used before, he marked out a spot several yards from the point at which he had been digging.

Again we set to work with the spades. I was dreadfully tired, but for some reason did not seem to mind the work this time. I had become interested, even excited. Perhaps there was something about Legrand which impressed me. I dug eagerly, and now and then caught myself actually looking with some expectation for the buried treasure. When we had been at work about an hour and a half, we were again interrupted by the violent howling of the dog. His noisiness had at first been merely playful, but he now seemed serious. When Jupiter again tried to muzzle him, he resisted furiously, and, leaping into the hole, tore up the dirt with his paws. In a few seconds he had uncovered a mass of human bones, forming two complete skeletons. One or two strokes of a spade upturned the head of a large Spanish knife and three or four loose pieces of gold and silver coin.

At the sight of these Jupiter was filled with excitement, but his master seemed extremely disappointed. He urged us, however, to continue digging. He had scarcely spoken the words when I stumbled and fell forward, having caught my toe in a large ring of iron that lay half buried in the loose earth.

We now worked in earnest. Never did I pass ten minutes of such tense excitement. During this time we dug up an oblong chest of wood, which must have been coated with something to preserve and harden it. This box was three feet and a half long, three feet wide, and two and a half feet deep. It was held together by bands of iron. On each side of the top were three rings of iron, six in all, by means of which it could be carried by six people. It was so heavy we could scarcely move it, and soon realized we couldn't possibly carry it away. Luckily, the lid was fastened with sliding bolts. We drew these back, trembling and panting with anxiety. In an instant a treasure of enormous value lay gleaming before us. As the rays of the lantern fell within the pit, a glow that dazzled our eyes flashed from a heap of gold and jewels.

I cannot describe my feelings. Surprise was the strongest, of course. Legrand seemed worn out with excitement and said little. Jupiter was as pale as it is possible for any Negro to be. He seemed absolutely thunderstruck. Presently he fell upon his knees in the pit and buried his arms up to the elbows in gold, as though he were bathing in it. Finally, with a deep sigh, he exclaimed,

"And dis all cum ob de goole-bug! Poor little goolebug what I hated so! Ain't you shamed of yourself, nigger? Answer me dat."

I reminded them both that they should find some way of removing the treasure. It was growing late, and we would have to work hard if we got everything housed before daylight. It was hard to plan, all our ideas being different. Finally we removed two-thirds of the contents of the box and thus were able to raise it from the hole. The articles taken out were hidden among the brambles, and the dog left to guard them. We then made for home with the chest, reaching the cabin in safety about one o'clock in the morning. Worn out as we were, it was impossible to do more right then. We had supper and rested until two, starting for the hills immediately afterward. With us we carried three heavy bags, which we had found at the cabin. A little before four we arrived at the pit, divided the remainder of the treasure among us, and, leaving the hole unfilled, carried our golden burdens to the cabin, arriving there just as the first streaks of dawn appeared.

We were now completely tired out, but too excited to sleep. After three or four hours of uneasy rest, we all got up to examine our treasure.

The chest had been full to the brim, and we spent the whole day and the greater part of the next night examining its contents. Nothing had been put in order. After sorting with care, we found we had even greater wealth than we had at first supposed. In coin there was more than four hundred and fifty thousand dollars, as far as we could estimate the value of the pieces. There was no silver. All was gold of an early date and a great variety: French, Spanish, and German money, with a few English guineas. There were several large and heavy coins so worn that we could not read their inscriptions. There was no American money.

The value of the jewels we found hard to figure. There were diamonds, a hundred and ten in all, and not one of them small; three hundred and ten emeralds, all very beautiful; and twenty-one sapphires and an opal. These stones had all been broken from their settings and thrown loose in the chest. The settings themselves, which we picked out from among the other gold, appeared to have been beaten up with a hammer to prevent identification.

Besides all this there was a quantity of solid gold ornaments—nearly two hundred finger and ear-rings, thirty rich chains, eighty-three very large and heavy crucifixes, a huge golden punch bowl, two sword-handles beautifully carved, and many smaller articles which I cannot remember. The weight of these valuables was more than three hundred and fifty pounds, and in this estimate I have not included one hundred and ninety-seven beautiful gold watches, three of them being worth five hundred dollars apiece. Many of them were very old, and useless as timekeepers; but all were richly jeweled and in cases of great worth. We estimated the entire contents of the chest that night at a million and a half dollars. When we later disposed of the treasure, keeping a few things for our own use, we found that we had greatly under-estimated its worth.

When we had at length concluded our examination, and the excitement had worn off a little, Legrand, who saw that I was dying with impatience to find out how he had solved the riddle, gave me a full explanation of everything.

"You remember," said he, "the night when I handed you the rough sketch I had made of the scarab, I was quite angry at you for insisting that my drawing resembled a skull. I thought you were joking, but afterward I remembered the peculiar spots on the back of the insect and wondered whether your remark might now have some cause. Still, I was a bit angry and, when you handed me the piece of parchment, was about to crumple it up and throw it on the fire."

"The scrap of paper, you mean," said I.

"No, it looked like paper, but when I came to draw on it, I discovered it to be a piece of very thin parchment. It was quite dirty, I remember. Well, as I was about to crumple it, I looked at the sketch, and you may imagine how surprised I was when I saw the figure of a skull just where, it seemed to me, I had made the drawing of the beetle. For a moment I was too amazed to think accurately. I took a candle and, seating myself at the other end of the room, examined the parchment more carefully. Then I realized that my own sketch, just as I had made it, was on the opposite side. I was amazed to realize that there had been a skull on the other side of the paper immediately beneath my figure of the scarab, and that the two drawings should resemble each other so closely.

"When I recovered from my surprise, I began to remember, positively, that there had been no drawing on the parchment when I made my sketch of the scarab. I was certain of this, for I remembered turning the paper over to find the cleanest spot. If the skull had been there, I could not have failed to notice it. Here was a mystery hard to explain, though the first faint glimmer of an idea began to come to me while you were still here.

"When you had gone and Jupiter was fast asleep, I started to investigate thoroughly. First I tried to remember where the parchment had come from. The spot where we discovered the scarab was on the coast of the mainland, about a mile east of the island and only a short distance above high water mark. When I took hold of it, it gave me a sharp bite, which caused me to let it drop. Jupiter, before grasping the insect, which had flown toward him, looked about for a leaf or something with which to hold it. At this moment we both saw the scrap of parchment, which I took for granted was paper. It was lying half-buried in the sand, a corner sticking up. Near the spot where we found it I saw the remains of the hull of what seemed to me a ship's long boat. The wreck must have been there for a long while, judging by its appearance.

"Well, Jupiter picked up the parchment, wrapped the beetle in it, and gave it to me. Soon afterward we turned to go home and on the way met Lieutenant G——. I showed him the insect, and he begged me to let him take it to the fort. I handed it to him, but kept the piece of parchment in which it had been wrapped.

"You remember that, when I went to the table for some paper, I found none where it is usually kept. I searched my pockets and chanced upon the parchment. The circumstances impressed me, somehow. I seemed to have put together two links of a great chain. There was a boat lying on the seacoast and not far from it a parchment—not a paper—with a skull on it, and the skull, or death's head, is the well-known emblem of the pirate.

"Parchment is durable, and it is used only for matters of great importance. The form of it was unusual too. Although one of its corners had been destroyed, it could be seen that the original shape was oblong. It was the sort of slip that would be chosen for a memorandum of something to be long remembered and carefully kept."

"But," I interrupted, "you say that the skull was not on the parchment when you made the drawing of the beetle."

"Ah, I had comparatively little difficulty solving this problem. You remember a fire was blazing on the hearth when you were here. Just as you began to look at the parchment, Wolf, the dog, entered and leaped upon you. With your left hand you petted him, while your right, holding the parchment, fell between your knees very close to the fire. Once I thought it might catch fire and was about to caution you, but before I could speak you were examining it again. Heat had brought to light on the parchment the drawing of the skull. You know that chemical preparations have existed for centuries by means of which it is possible to write so that letters can be seen only when heat is applied.

"So after you had gone, I held every bit of the parchment close to the glowing heat. Then I saw not only the skull, but at the corner of the slip a figure which I saw was intended to be a kid. Now you may have heard of one Captain Kidd. It seemed to me that the animal was intended as a sort of signature, and the skull a stamp or seal, though as yet there was no letter or message in evidence.

"Anyway, I began to see great good fortune coming my way. Perhaps it was rather a desire than an actual belief. I think Jupiter's silly words about the bug being of solid gold had an effect on my imagination."

"Proceed," said I. "I am all impatience."

"You have heard, of course, the many stories about money buried on the Atlantic coast by Kidd and his companions. These rumors have gone on so long I felt they must have some basis in fact. Apparently no one had ever found any of the money. I wondered if some loss of a memorandum indicating its location might not have been the cause of its remaining buried. Have you ever heard of any being found?"

"Never."

"Everyone knows that Kidd accumulated a vast fortune. I had a hope, nearly a certainty, that the parchment held a record of the hiding-place."

"How did you proceed?"

"I carefully rinsed the parchment by pouring warm water over it, and then placed it in a tin pan with the skull downward. I put the pan over the fire and, when it had become thoroughly heated, took out the parchment and found it spotted in several places with figures arranged in lines. Then I heated it again and found I had made everything clear."

Here Legrand showed me the following cryptogram.

53‡‡†305))6*;4826)4‡.)4‡);806*;48†8¶60))85;;]8*;:‡*8†83(88)5*†;
46(;88*96*?;8)*‡(;485);5*†2:*‡(;4956*2(5*—4)8¶8*;4069285);)6†8)
4‡‡;1(‡9;48081;8:8‡1;48†85;4)485†528806*81(‡9;48;(88;4(‡?34;48)4‡;
161;:188;‡?;

"But," I said, "I am as much in the dark as ever. How could you possibly solve this?"

"The solution isn't nearly as difficult as you might imagine," said Legrand. "These figures are a cipher, of course, and, from what is known of Kidd, I realized it couldn't possibly be a very difficult one."

"And you really solved it?"

"Readily; I have solved others ten thousand times harder, since I've always taken an interest in such things and doubt whether they can be made too hard to be solved by a person really determined to succeed.

"First, the language of the cipher has to be determined. In this case it was easy to see that it must be in English, because of the drawing of the kid to signify Captain Kidd. That wouldn't have been understandable in any other language.

"You can see there are no divisions between words. That made my task harder, too. So my first step was to figure out the numbers and characters which occur most often. I counted them and discovered something like this: 8 occurs thirty-three times; there are 26 semicolons; 4 occurs nineteen times, etc.

"In English *E* is used more than any other letter. It is practically impossible to find a sentence of any length in which it doesn't occur very often. In Kidd's cipher the number 8 is most frequent. I started, then, by taking it for granted that 8 stood for the letter *e.*

"Now, of all words in the language *the* is most used. In the cipher we find in seven places an arrangement of three characters, *;48*. If the semicolon represents t, then 4 is h and 8 is e. That gave me not only three letters and a single word, but also a clue to the beginnings and endings of other words. Look, for example, at the next to the last *;48* in the cipher. We know that the semicolon is the start of a word, and we know five of the six following letters. That, leaving a space for the one we don't know, give us *t-eeth.* We can easily figure that the *th* belongs in the next word, for no letter will fit in the space left. So we take out the *th* and have left *t-ee.* Going through the alphabet, we find that only *r* will fit in. Thus we have the word *tree,* and we know that *r* is represented by *(*.

"In this manner I proceeded until I had found the meaning of each symbol in the cryptogram and so could decipher it all. But you would not care to hear all the details, I'm sure. Let us hurry on to the message itself. Here it is:

"*A good glass in the bishop's hostel in the devil's seat forty-one degrees and thirteen minutes northeast and by north main branch seventh limb east side shoot from the left eye of the skull a bee line from the tree through the shot fifty feet out.*"

"But," said I, "the puzzle seems as great as ever. How could you possibly make sense of all that?"

"I confess," replied Legrand, "that it does all seem confused. My first task was to find some natural divisions in it."

"You mean to punctuate it?"

"Something of that sort."

"How could you possibly do that?"

"That was the easiest thing of all to do. It seems to fall into natural divisions. When I had finally worked it out, it read as follows:

*"A good glass in the Bishop's hostel in the Devil's seat—forty-one degrees and thirteen minutes—Northeast and by North—main branch seventh limb east side—shoot from the left eye of the skull—a bee-line from the tree through the shot fifty feet out."*

"Even this," said I, "leaves me still in the dark."

"It left me in the dark, too," said Legrand, "for several days, during which I inquired in the neighborhood of Sullivan's Island for any building called the 'Bishop's Hotel,' for of course I didn't use the old word 'hostel'. One morning it suddenly occurred to me that 'Bishop's Hostel' might refer to an old family of Bessop, which for a great many years had lived in an ancient manor-house about four miles north of the island. So I went over to the plantation and inquired among the older Negroes on the place. One of the oldest of them said she had heard of such a place as Bessop's Castle, but that it was not a castle, but a rock.

"With her I found the place easily, and, after dismissing her, examined it carefully. The 'castle' was made of a number of cliffs and rocks, one of which was remarkably high and unusual in appearance. I climbed to the top of it and then wondered what to do next. Suddenly my eyes fell upon a narrow ledge on the eastern face of the rock a yard below the summit on which I stood. This ledge stuck out about eighteen inches and was not more than a foot wide, while a niche in the cliff just above it made it resemble a hollow-backed chair. I was sure this was the 'devil's seat.'

"The good glass I knew would be a telescope. I hurried home for one and then returned to the rock. I let myself down to the ledge and found that it was possible to sit on it in only one position. I was sure that the phrase 'forty-one degrees and thirteen minutes' gave directions for leveling the glass above the visible horizon, since the words 'north-east and by north' indicated a horizontal direction. Using a pocket-compass and pointing the glass according to direction, I moved the telescope cautiously up or down until I noticed a circular opening in the foliage of a tree much higher than all the others around it. In the center of this opening I saw a white spot, but could not at first tell what it was. Adjusting the telescope again, I saw that it was a human skull.

"By that time I thought I had solved the mystery entirely; for the phrase 'main branch, seventh limb, east side', could refer only to the position of the skull on the tree, while 'shoot from the left eye of the skull' seemed to mean that a bullet should be dropped from the left eye of the skull, and a straight line be drawn from the nearest point of the trunk through the spot the bullet fell, and then extended a distance of fifty feet. That would give a very definite location, and I thought it at least possible that a treasure was concealed there."

"All this," I said, "is very clear and simple. It surely shows your cleverness, though. What happened after you left the Bishop's Hotel?"

"I started homeward. The instant I left 'the devil's seat', however, the circular opening disappeared. I couldn't get a glimpse of it afterward, either. The circular opening can be seen from no other point than the narrow ledge on which I had sat.

"Jupiter had gone with me to the Bishop's Hostel, but the next day I got up very early and managed to slip out without his seeing me in order to search for the tree. After a long while I found it. You know what happened after that."

"I suppose," I said, "you missed the spot, when we first dug, through Jupiter's mistake in letting the bug fall through the right eye instead of through the left eye of the skull."

"Exactly. That made a difference of about two inches and a half in the spot where we first began to measure. Of course this distance increased as we advanced, and by the time we had gone fifty feet we were entirely off the track. If I hadn't been perfectly sure there was treasure buried somewhere, we might have had all our work for nothing."

"I suppose the idea of letting a bullet fall through a skull's eye was suggested to Kidd by the pirates' flag. He probably thought it would be a very suitable way to start looking for treasure."

"Perhaps so; but there was a common-sense reason, too. In order to be seen it was necessary that the object be white; and there is nothing like a human skull for keeping and even increasing its whiteness in all kinds of weather."

"But your queer actions about the beetle? I thought surely you were mad. And why did you insist on Jupiter's letting the beetle instead of a bullet down from the skull?"

"I was annoyed at you for doubting my sanity. So I resolved to punish you a bit by puzzling you. For this reason I attached so much importance to the beetle. A remark of yours about the weight suggested to me the idea of using it in place of a bullet."

"I can see your point. And now there is only one thing which puzzles me. How can we explain the skeletons found in the hole?"

"You know as much about that as I do. There seems to be only one way of accounting for them—a dreadful one. Kidd must have had help in burying the treasure. He probably thought it unwise to have anyone alive who knew his secret. A couple of blows with a pick could have killed his helpers while they were busy digging the pit. Then the secret was forever safe—until you and I came along."

# THE MURDERS IN THE RUE MORGUE

RESIDING in Paris during the spring and part of the summer of 18–, I there became acquainted with a Monsieur C. Auguste Dupin. This young gentleman was of an excellent family, but by a variety of unusual events had been reduced to such poverty that he had lost his ambition and had ceased to mingle with people or to care for the recovery of his fortune. There still remained in his possession, however, a small remnant of his inheritance; and with the income from this he managed, by strict economy, to procure the necessaries of life, without troubling himself about its luxuries. Books, indeed, were his sole extravagance, and in Paris these are easily obtained.

Our first meeting was at an out-of-the-way library in the Rue[1] Montmartre, where we were both in search of the same very rare book. We saw each other again and again. I was deeply interested in his family history, which he related to me with frankness. I was astonished, too, at the vast extent of his reading, and, above all, I felt my soul kindled by the wild and vivid freshness of his imagination. I felt that the society of such a man would be to me a treasure beyond price; and this feeling I frankly confided to him. It was at length arranged that we should live together during my stay in the city. As my financial state was better than his, I was permitted to pay for the renting and furnishing, in a style which suited our gloomy mood, of a queer old house. This dwelling, long deserted and falling into decay, stood in a lonely and desolate portion of the Faubourg St. Germain.[2]

If the routine of our life at this place had been known to the world, we should probably have been regarded as madmen—although harmless ones. Our privacy was perfect. We admitted no visitors. Indeed, the place of our retirement had been carefully kept a secret from my own former associates; and it had been many years since Dupin had ceased to know or to be known in Paris. We existed for ourselves alone.

It was a freak of fancy in my friend to love the night; and into this whim, as into all his others, I quietly fell, giving myself up to his habits completely. Of course

[1] Rue—street.

[2] Faubourg St. Germain—a suburb of Paris outside the old city walls.

Night would not stay with us always; but we could imitate her presence. At the first dawn of the morning we closed all the shutters of our old building and lighted candles, which, strongly perfumed, threw out the ghastliest and feeblest of rays. By the aid of these, we busied ourselves in dreams—reading, writing, or conversing, until warned by the clock of the arrival of the true Darkness. Then we sallied forth into the streets, arm in arm, and roamed far and wide until a late hour, amid the wild lights and shadows of the crowded city.

At such times I could not help noticing and admiring a peculiar mind-reading ability of Dupin. He seemed, too, to take an eager delight in using it. He boasted to me, with a low chuckling laugh, that most men, in relation to himself, wore windows in their bosoms, and he was accustomed to follow up such assertions by direct and startling proofs of his intimate knowledge of my own thoughts and feelings. His manner at these moments was cold and far away; his eyes were vacant in expression; while his voice, usually a rich tenor, rose to a higher pitch.

An instance of Dupin's mind-reading ability occurred one night when we were strolling down a long, dirty street in the vicinity of the Palais Royal.[1] Being both apparently occupied with thought, neither of us had spoken a syllable for fifteen minutes at least. All at once Dupin broke forth with these words: "He is a very little fellow, that's true, and would be a better actor for a variety show."

[1] Palais Royal—a royal palace built about 1630, now a public building.

"There can be no doubt of that," I replied absent-mindedly, not at first observing (so much had I been lost in thought) the extraordinary manner in which the speaker had read my mind. An instant afterward I recollected myself, and my astonishment was complete.

"Dupin," said I gravely, "this is beyond my comprehension. I am amazed and can scarcely credit my senses. How was it possible you should know I was thinking of —?" Here I paused to find out beyond a doubt whether he really knew of whom I was thinking.

"Of Chantilly," said he. "Why do you pause? You were remarking to yourself that his small figure unfitted him for a tragic role."

This was exactly what had formed the subject of my thoughts. Chantilly was a one-time shoemaker, who, becoming stage-struck, had attempted to play the part of the hero Xerxes in a tragedy and had made a notorious failure of it.

"Tell me, for Heaven's sake," I exclaimed, "the method by which you have been able to read my mind in this matter." I was even more startled than I would have been willing to express.

There are few persons who have not, at some period of their lives, amused themselves in retracing the mental steps by which they have come to some particular conclusion. By association of thoughts one idea leads to another, until there is a vast distance and difference between the starting point and the finish.

By some such method had Dupin read my thoughts. A grocer who ran against me in the street and caused me to stub the toe of my shoe had reminded me of the shoe-maker. The fact that I was thinking of him was shown by my glancing at the constellation Orion, which had been mentioned in a recent review of the shoe-maker's play. The same article had ridiculed the shoe-maker's small size. Dupin noticed that I smiled. He saw, too, that instead of walking with my usual stooping gait, I had now drawn myself erect. This happened when I thought of the small figure of the shoemaker. All of this had been observed by Dupin, with his resulting startling remark. Later I remembered all this, when he astonished the Paris police just as he had astonished me that night.

Not long after this, we were looking over an evening edition of the "Gazette de Tribunaux" when the following paragraphs arrested our attention:

"Extraordinary Murders:—This morning, about three o'clock, the inhabitants of the Quartier St. Roch were roused from sleep by a succession of terrific shrieks, issuing, apparently, from the fourth story of a house in the Rue Morgue, known to be occupied only by one Madame L'Espanaye and her daughter, Mademoiselle Camille L'Espanaye. After some delay the gateway was broken in and eight or ten of the neighbors entered, accompanied by two policemen. By this time the cries had ceased; but, as the party rushed up the first flight of stairs, two or more rough voices, in angry tones, which seemed to come from the upper part of the house, could be heard. As the second landing was reached, these sounds, too, had ceased, and everything remained perfectly quiet. Upon arriving at a large back chamber in the fourth story, the party forced the door, which was found locked, with the key inside. Within was a sight which struck every one present with horror and astonishment.

"The apartment was in the wildest disorder—the furniture broken and thrown about in all directions. There was only one bedstead; from this the bed had been removed and thrown into the middle of the floor. On a chair lay a razor, smeared with blood. On the hearth were two or three long and thick locks of human hair, also dabbled with blood and apparently pulled out by the roots. Upon the floor were three large silver spoons, an earring of topaz, and two bags containing nearly four thousand francs[1] in gold. Bureau drawers had apparently been robbed, though many articles still remained in them. A small iron safe was discovered under the bed. It was open, with the key still in the lock, but had no contents beyond a few old papers and letters of no consequence.

"Of Madame L'Espanaye no traces were seen; but a quantity of soot being observed in the fire-place, a search was made in the chimney. Horrible to relate, the corpse of the daughter, head downward, was dragged out, it having been forced up the narrow space for some distance. The body was still quite warm. There were many severe scratches on the face, and on the throat

[1] A *franc* at the time of this story was worth 20 cents.

dark bruises and deep indentations of finger nails, as if the deceased had been choked to death.

"In a small paved yard in the rear of the building lay the corpse of the old lady, with her throat so entirely cut that, upon an attempt to raise her, the head fell off. The body, as well as the head, was fearfully mutilated—the former so much so as to seem scarcely human.

"To this horrible mystery there is not as yet, we believe, the slightest clue."

The next day's paper had these additional particulars: "The Tragedy in the Rue Morgue—Many individuals have been examined in relation to this most extraordinary and frightful affair, but nothing whatever has happened to throw light upon it. We give all the testimony so far collected.

"Pauline Dubourg, laundress, testifies that she has known both the deceased for three years, having washed for them during that period. The old lady and her daughter seemed on good terms with each other. They were excellent pay. She had heard a rumor that Madame L. told fortunes for her living and had money put by. She had never met any person in the house when she called for or delivered clothes. There was no servant in the house and no furniture in any part of the building except the fourth story.

"Pierre Moreau, tobacconist, testifies that he has been in the habit of sending small quantities of tobacco and snuff to Madame L. for nearly four years. The deceased and her daughter had occupied the house, which belonged to them, for six years. The old lady was childish. The witness had seen the daughter five or six times during the six years. The two lived an exceedingly retired life, though supposed to have money. He did not believe the rumor that Madame L. told fortunes. He had never seen any person enter the door except the old lady and her daughter, a janitor once or twice, and a doctor some eight or ten times.

"Many other neighbors gave the same evidence. No one frequented the house. It was not known whether there were any living relatives of Madame L. and her daughter. The shutters on the front windows were seldom opened. Those in the rear were always closed, with the exception of the large back room in the fourth story.

"Isidore Musét, policeman, witnesses that he was called to the house about three o'clock in the morning and found some twenty or thirty persons at the gateway, trying to get in. The shrieks continued until the gate was forced, and then suddenly ceased. They seemed to be screams of some person or persons in great agony. They were loud and drawn out, not short and quick. Upon reaching the first landing, he heard two loud and angry voices, the one gruff, the other much shriller—a very strange voice. The former was apparently that of a Frenchman. He was positive it was not a woman's voice. The shrill voice was that of a foreigner. He could not be sure whether it was that of a man or a woman. The words were not distinguishable, but sounded like Spanish.

"Henri Duval, a neighbor, testifies that he was one of

the party who first entered the house. He agrees with the testimony of Musét in general, but thinks that the shrill voice was that of an Italian, though he could not make out the words spoken. The voice might have been a woman's. Duval had frequently talked with Madame L. and her daughter and knew that the shrill voice was not that of either of them.

"——— Odenheimer, restaurant proprietor, volunteered his testimony. Not speaking French, he was examined through an interpreter. He is a native of Amsterdam, who was passing the house at the time and heard the shrieks, which he described as awful and distressing. They lasted for perhaps ten minutes. He disagrees with the previous evidence in only one respect. He was sure that the shrill voice was that of a man—a Frenchman. He could not distinguish the words. They were loud and quick, unequal, spoken apparently in fear as well as anger. The voice was more harsh than shrill. The gruff voice said repeatedly, 'The devil,' and once, 'My God.'

"Jules Mignaud, the banker, says Madame L'Espanaye had some property and made frequent deposits in small sums. The third day before her death she took out in person the sum of four thousand francs. This was paid in gold, and a clerk sent home with the money.

"Adolphe Le Bon, bank clerk, testifies that on the day in question, about noon, he accompanied Madame L. to her home with the four thousand francs put up in two bags. When the door was opened, Mademoiselle L. appeared and took from his hand one of the bags, while the old lady relieved him of the other. He then bowed and departed. He did not see any person in the street at the time. It is a by-street and very lonely.

"William Bird, tailor, was one of the party who entered the house. He is an Englishman who has lived in Paris two years. He heard the two voices and is sure that the gruff one was that of a Frenchman. He could make out several words, but cannot remember them all. There was a sound as of several people struggling—a scraping and scuffling sound. The shrill voice was very loud—louder than the gruff one. He is sure that it was not the voice of an Englishman. It appeared to be that of a German. It might have been a woman's voice. He does not understand German.

"Four of the above-named witnesses, being recalled, say that the door of the room in which was found the body of Mademoiselle L. was locked on the inside when the party reached it. Everything was perfectly silent—no groans or noises of any kind. No person was seen. The windows, of both the back and the front room, were down and firmly fastened from within. The door leading from the front room into the passage was locked, with the key on the inside. There was not an inch of any portion of the house which was not carefully searched. The time elapsing between the hearing of the voices and the breaking open of the room door was variously estimated by the witnesses. Some made it as short as three minutes—some as long as five. The door was opened with difficulty.

"Alfonzo Garcia, undertaker, a native of Spain, was

one of those who entered the house. He heard the voices in dispute. The gruff voice was that of a Frenchman, and the shrill voice was that of an Englishman. He is sure of this, although he does not understand the English language.

"Alberto Montani, confectioner, testifies that he was among the first to ascend the stairs. He says the gruff voice was that of a Frenchman. He distinguished several words. The speaker appeared to be arguing. He could not make out the words of the shrill voice. He thinks it was a Russian. He himself is an Italian and has never conversed with a Russian.

"Several witnesses, recalled, here testified that the chimneys of all the rooms on the fourth floor were too narrow to admit the passage of a human being. There is no back passage by which anyone could have escaped while the party proceeded up stairs. The body of Mademoiselle L'Espanaye was so firmly wedged in the chimney that it could not be got down until four or five of the party united their strength.

"Paul Dumas, physician, says that he was called to view the bodies about daybreak. They were both then lying on the sacking of the bedstead in the chamber where Mademoiselle L. was found. The corpse of the young lady was much bruised and scratched. The fact that it had been thrust up the chimney would sufficiently account for this. The throat was greatly chafed. There were deep scratches just below the chin, together with a series of black and blue spots, which were evidently the impression of fingers. The face was fearfully discolored, and the eyeballs protruded. The tongue had been partially bitten through. A large bruise was discovered upon the pit of the stomach, produced, apparently, by the pressure of a knee. In the opinion of Monsieur Dumas, Mademoiselle L'Espanaye had been choked to death by some person or persons unknown. The corpse of the mother was horribly mutilated. The whole body was dreadfully bruised and discolored. It is not possible to say how the injuries had been inflicted. A heavy club of wood or a broad bar of iron, a chair, or any large, heavy, and blunt weapon could have produced such results if wielded by the hands of a powerful man. No woman could have inflicted the blows with any weapon. The head of the deceased, when seen by the witness, was entirely separated from the body and greatly shattered. The throat had evidently been cut with some very sharp instrument—probably with a razor.

"Nothing further of importance was found, though several other persons were examined. A murder so mysterious and so perplexing was never before committed in Paris—if indeed a murder has been committed at all. The police are entirely at sea, an unusual occurrence in affairs of this nature. There is not, however, a shadow of a clue apparent."

The evening edition of the *Gazette* stated that the greatest excitement still continued in the Quartier St. Roch. The premises had been carefully re-searched and fresh examinations of witnesses started, but all to no purpose. A postscript, however, mentioned that

Adolphe Le Bon had been arrested and imprisoned, although nothing appeared to prove his guilt beyond the facts already detailed.

Dupin seemed singularly interested in the progress of this affair—at least so I judged from his manner, for he made no comments. It was only after the announcement that Le Bon had been imprisoned that he asked me my opinion about the murders. I could only agree with all Paris that there seemed no possibility of tracing the murderer.

"We must not judge," said Dupin, "by this shell of an examination. The Parisian police, so much praised for keenness, are clever, but no more. The results attained by them are often surprising, but, for the most part, are brought about by simple patience and thoroughness. When these qualities are insufficient, their schemes fail. As for these murders, let us make some examination for ourselves before we form an opinion about them. An inquiry will afford us amusement," (I thought this an odd term to use, but said nothing) "and besides, Le Bon once rendered me a service for which I am grateful. We will go and see the premises with our own eyes. I know G., the Prefect of Police, and shall have no difficulty in obtaining the necessary permission."

The permission obtained, we proceeded at once to the Rue Morgue. It was late in the afternoon when we reached it, as this quarter is at a great distance from that in which we lived. The house was easily found, for there were still many persons gazing up at the closed shutters with curiosity. Before going in, we walked up the street, turned down an alley, and then, again turning, passed in the rear of the building. Dupin, meanwhile, was examining the whole neighborhood with a closeness of attention for which I could see no possible reason.

Retracing our steps, we came again to the front of the dwelling, rang the bell, and, having presented our credentials to the officer in charge, were admitted to the house. We went up stairs to the chamber where the body of Mademoiselle L'Espanaye had been found and where both the corpses still lay. The disorder of the room had been left untouched. I saw nothing beyond what had been stated in the newspaper. Dupin, however, examined everything—not excepting the bodies of the victims. We then went into the other rooms and into the yard, a policeman accompanying us throughout. The examination occupied us until dark, when we took our departure. On our way home my companion stepped in for a moment at the office of one of the daily papers.

I have said that the whims of my friend were numerous. It was his humor now to decline all conversation on the subject of the murder until noon the next day. He then asked me if I had noticed anything *peculiar* at the scene of the crime. There was something in the manner of his emphasizing the word "peculiar" that made me shudder, I know not why.

"No, nothing *peculiar,*" I said. "Nothing more, at least, than we both saw stated in the paper."

"The *Gazette,*" he replied, "has not entered into the

unusual horror of the thing. It appears to me that this mystery is considered impossible to solve for the very reason which should cause it to be regarded as easy of solution—I mean for the outlandish character of it. The police are confused by the seeming absence of motive —not for the murder itself but for the atrocity of the murder. They are puzzled, too, by the voices heard in dispute, since no one was discovered upstairs but the assassinated Mademoiselle L'Espanaye; for there was no way of getting out without the notice of the party ascending. The wild disorder of the room; the corpse thrust, with the head downward, up the chimney; the frightful mutilation of the body of the old lady—all of these have paralyzed the mental powers of the government agents. They have fallen into the great but common error of confusing the unusual with the obscure."

I stared at the speaker with astonishment.

"I am now awaiting," continued he, looking toward the door of our apartment, " a person who, although not perhaps the actual performer of the butcheries, must have been in some measure involved in them. He is probably innocent of the worst portion of the crimes committed. I look for the man here—in this room—every moment. It is true that he may not arrive; but the probability is that he will. Should he come, it will be necessary to hold him. Here are pistols. We both know how to use them when occasion demands."

I took the pistols, scarcely knowing what I did, or believing what I heard, while Dupin went on, very much as if talking to himself. I have already spoken of his manner at such times. His words were addressed to me; but his voice, although by no means loud, had that tone which is commonly used in speaking to some one at a great distance. His eyes, vacant in expression, looked only at the wall.

"The voices heard in dispute," he said, "were not the voices of the women themselves. This was fully proved by the evidence. We are, therefore, sure that the old lady could not have destroyed her daughter first and then committed suicide. Anyway, Madame L'Espanaye would not have been strong enough to thrust her daughter's corpse up the chimney; nor could she have inflicted on herself the wounds of which she died. Murder, then, has been committed by some third party. Did you observe anything peculiar in the testimony of the witnesses?"

I remarked that, while all the witnesses agreed that the gruff voice was that of a Frenchman, there was much disagreement in regard to the shrill or harsh voice.

"That was the odd thing about the evidence," said Dupin. "The witnesses, as you remark, agreed unanimously about the gruff voice. In regard to the shrill voice, it is not so peculiar that they disagreed as it is that an Italian, an Englishman, a Spaniard, a Hollander, and a Frenchman all attempted to describe it as that of a foreigner. Each one is sure that it was not the voice of one of his own countrymen. How strange indeed must that voice have been! Notice these points. The voice is termed by one witness as 'harsh rather than shrill.' No words—no sounds resembling words—were understood by any witness.

"Now let us consider the room. What shall we first seek here? The means of escape used by the murderers. We are not believers in the supernatural. We know that the two women were not destroyed by spirits. Then how? The assassins were in the room where Mademoiselle L'Espanaye was found, or in the adjoining room, when the party ascended the stairs. It is only from these two rooms that we have to seek a way out. No *secret* way could have escaped the police. Not trusting to their eyes, I examined with my own. There were *no* secret ways out. The chimneys will not admit, all the way up, even the small body of a cat. Only the windows, and the ones on the back at that, remain as possibilities.

"There are two windows in the chamber. One is unobstructed by furniture and is wholly visible. The lower part of the other is hidden from view by the head of the bedstead, which is pushed up close against it. Both windows were securely fastened from within by a very stout nail hammered nearly to its head. I stepped to the unobstructed casement, withdrew the nail with some difficulty, and attempted to raise the sash. It resisted all my efforts, as I had expected.

"Yet I knew the murderers *did* escape from one of these windows, even though the sashes *were* fastened tight when the police examined them. They must, then, have the power of fastening themselves. A hidden spring, I knew, must exist. A careful search soon brought it to light. I pressed it and found that it worked.

"I now replaced the nail and examined it, attentively. A person passing out through this window might have reclosed it and the spring would have caught—but the nail could not have been replaced. This conclusion again narrowed the field of my investigation. The assassin *must* have escaped through the *other* window. If, then, the springs upon each sash were the same, as was probable, there *must* be a difference between the nails or their fixtures.

"Getting up on the bedstead, I looked over the head board carefully at the second window. Passing my hand down the board, I readily discovered and pressed the spring, which was, as I supposed, exactly like its neighbor. I now looked at the nail. It was as strong as the other, and apparently fitted in the same manner—driven in nearly up to the head.

"Upon this nail depended, then, the solution of this part of the mystery. 'There *must* be something wrong,' I said, 'about the nail.' I touched it, and the head came off in my fingers. The rest of it remained in the hole where it had been broken off. The break was an old one and had apparently been done by the blow of a hammer, which had partially buried the head of the nail in the top of the bottom sash. I carefully replaced this head portion in the hollow from which I had taken it, and the resemblance to a perfect nail was complete, the split being invisible. Pressing the spring, I raised the sash a few inches; the head, remaining firmly in its bed, went up with it. I closed the window, and the nail appeared whole.

"The riddle, so far, was now solved. The assassins had escaped through the window at the head of the bed. Dropping of its own accord upon their exit, or perhaps purposely closed, it had become fastened by its spring. The police had then mistaken the hold of the spring for that of the nail.

"The next problem was the way the murderer climbed down. I had found that out in my walks with you around the building. About five and a half feet from the window in question there runs a lightning rod. From this it would have been impossible for anyone to reach the window itself, to say nothing of entering it. I observed, however, that the shutters of the fourth story were of a peculiar kind. They are in the form of an ordinary door, except that the lower half is latticed, thus affording an excellent hold for the hands. In width they are fully three feet and a half. When we saw them from the rear of the house, they were both about half open.

"Although the police had evidently overlooked this, it was clear to me that the shutter belonging to the window at the head of the bed would, if swung fully back to the wall, reach to within two feet of the lightning rod. It was evident also that anyone with an unusual degree of agility and courage might have entered the window in this way.

"I wish you to bear especially in mind that I have spoken of a *very* unusual degree of activeness as necessary to the success of so difficult a feat. I want to show you first that the thing might have been accomplished; but second and chiefly the abnormal agility which could accomplish it. I want you to connect that *very unusual* agility with that *very* peculiar shrill (or harsh) and *unequal* voice about whose nationality no two persons could agree and in whose speech no word could be detected."

At these words a dim and half-formed idea of the meaning of Dupin flitted through my mind. I seemed at the very brink of understanding.

"You will see," my friend went on, "that I have shifted the question from one of exit to that of entrance. I want to convey the idea that they were both made in the same way. Now let us look at the inside of the room. Though the bureau drawers had been disordered, many articles of clothing still remained in them. How are we to know then that any articles were actually taken? Perhaps the drawers contained no more to start with. Madame L'Espanaye and her daughter lived a very retired life. They would have needed few changes of clothing. If a thief had taken anything, why had he not taken all? Why, also, did he leave four thousand francs in gold? We know that the gold *was* abandoned, for almost the entire sum mentioned by the banker was still there. I wish you to discard the blundering idea of the police that robbery was a motive. To me it is no more than a coincidence that the murders should have been committed three days after a large sum of money was delivered at the house.

"Keeping steadily in mind the points to which I have called your attention, that peculiar voice, that unusual agility, and that startling absence of motive in a murder so horrible, let us glance at the butchery itself. Here is a woman strangled to death and thrust up a chimney head downward. Ordinary assassins, even the most brutal of them, never commit murders like this or dispose of corpses in such a way. Think, too, how great must have been the strength which could have thrust the body up an opening so forcibly that several persons could scarcely drag it down.

"On the hearth were very thick locks of gray human hair, which had been torn out by the roots. You are aware of the great force necessary to tear from the head even twenty or thirty hairs together. You saw these locks in question. Their roots were clotted with bits of the flesh of the scalp—sure proof of the enormous power which had been exerted in uprooting half a million hairs at a time. The throat of the old lady was not merely cut, but the head absolutely separated from the body; the weapon was a mere razor. I wish you to look at the brutal force of these deeds.

"If, now, in addition to all these things, you have thought of the odd disorder of the room, we can combine an astounding agility, a superhuman strength, a brutal fierceness, a butchery without motive, and a voice foreign in tone to the ears of men of many nations and lacking in any distinct syllables. What, then, is the result? What impressions have they made upon your imagination?"

I felt my flesh creep as Dupin asked me the question. "A madman," I said, "has done this deed—some raving maniac escaped from a neighboring asylum."

"In some respects," he replied, "your idea is not far from the truth. But madmen are of some nation, and their language, no matter how wild, has always understandable syllables. Besides, the hair of a madman is not like this. I pried this little tuft loose from the stiff fingers of Madame L'Espanaye. What can you make of it?"

"Dupin!" I said, completely unnerved, "this is no *human* hair."

"I have not said that it is," said he, "but before you decide, look at this paper. It is a drawing of what has been described in one portion of the testimony as dark bruises and deep indentations of finger nails upon the throat of Mademoiselle L'Espanaye, and in another as a series of livid spots, evidently the impression of fingers.

"You will see," continued my friend, "that this drawing gives the idea of a firm and fixed hold. There is no *slipping* apparent. Attempt, now, to place all your fingers at the same time in the impression as you see them."

I made the attempt in vain. "This," I said, "is the mark of no human hand."

"Read now," replied Dupin, "this passage from Cuvier."

It was a minute account of the large yellow Ourang-Outang[1] of the East Indian Islands. The gigantic size, the vast strength, the wild fierceness, and the imitative

[1] Ourang-outang or orang-utan—a heavy, red-haired ape of the forests of Borneo and Sumatra.

powers of these animals are well known to all. I understood the full horrors of the murder at once.

"The description of the fingers," said I, "is in exact agreement with this drawing. This tuft of hair, too, is identical in character with this beast. But I am still bewildered about the details of this frightful mystery. Besides, there were two voices heard, and one of them was definitely that of a Frenchman."

"True; and you will remember an expression heard by all the witnesses—the expression 'Mon Dieu.'[1] Upon these two words, therefore, I have mainly built my hopes of a full solution of the riddle. A Frenchman knew about the murder. Possibly he was innocent of all share in the bloody affair. The Ourang-Outang may have escaped from him. He may have traced it to the room of the murder but have been unable to recapture it. It may be still at large. I will not go on with these guesses, for they are really little more than that. If the Frenchman in question is really innocent of the crime, this advertisement, which I left last night, on our way home, at the office of *Le Monde* (a paper devoted to the shipping interest and much read by sailors), will bring him here."

He handed me a paper, and I read this:

> "Caught—In the Bois de Boulogne, early in the morning of the —— (the morning of the murder) a very large, yellow Ourang-Outang of the Bornese species. The owner (a sailor on a Maltese vessel)

[1] My God.

may have the animal again by identifying it satisfactorily and paying a few charges for its capture and keeping. Call at No. —, Rue —, Faubourg St. Germain — at three."

"How could you possibly know," I asked, "that the man was a sailor and one belonging to a Maltese vessel?"

"I do not know it," said Dupin, "and I am not sure of it. Here, however, is a small piece of ribbon, which from its form and from its greasy appearance has evidently been used in tying the hair in one of those long pigtails of which sailors are so fond. Moreover, this knot is one which few but sailors could tie, and is peculiar to the Maltese. I picked the ribbon up at the foot of the lightning rod. It could not have belonged to either of the dead women."

At this moment we heard a step upon the stairs.

"Be ready," said Dupin, "with your pistols, but do not show them without a signal from me."

The front door of the house had been left open, and the visitor had entered without ringing and advanced several steps upon the staircase. Now, however, he seemed to hesitate. Presently we heard him going down. Dupin was moving quickly to the door, when we again heard him coming up. He did not turn back a second time, but stepped up with decision and rapped on the door of our room.

"Come in," said Dupin in a cheerful and hearty tone.

A man entered. He was evidently a sailor—a tall, stout, and muscular-looking person, with a certain attractive, dare-devil expression. His face, greatly sunburned, was more than half hidden by whiskers and a mustache. He had with him a huge club, but appeared to be otherwise unarmed.

"Sit down, my friend," said Dupin. "I suppose you have called about the Ourang-Outang. I envy you the possession of him. A fine and no doubt a valuable animal. How old do you suppose him to be?"

The sailor drew a deep breath, with the air of a man relieved of a heavy burden, and then replied in an assured tone, "I have no way of telling, but he can't be more than four or five years old. Have you got him here?"

"Oh, no; we have no conveniences for keeping him here. He is at a livery stable nearby. You can get him in the morning. Of course you are prepared to identify the property?"

"To be sure I am, sir."

"I shall be sorry to part with him," said Dupin.

"I don't mean that you should be at all this trouble for nothing, sir. I'm very willing to pay a reward—anything in reason."

"Well," replied my friend, "that is all very fair, to be sure. Let me think!—what should I have? Oh! I'll tell you. Give me all the information you have about these murders in the Rue Morgue."

Dupin said the last words very quietly. Just as quietly, too, he walked toward the door, locked it, and put the key in his pocket. He then drew out his pistol and placed it upon the table.

The sailor's face flushed. He started to his feet and grasped his club; but the next moment he fell back into his seat, trembling violently. I pitied him from the bottom of my heart.

"My friend," said Dupin in a kind tone, "you are alarming yourself without cause. We mean you no harm whatever. I know that you are innocent of the crimes in the Rue Morgue. It will not do, however, to deny that you are in some way connected with them. Now the thing stands thus. You have done nothing which you could have avoided. You haven't even robbed, when you could have done so readily. You have nothing to conceal. On the other hand, you are bound by every principle of honor to confess all you know. An innocent man is now in prison, charged with the crime which you can solve."

The sailor had recovered his presence of mind while Dupin said this, but his original boldness was all gone.

"So help me God!" said he after a brief pause, "I will tell you all I know about this affair, but I do not expect you to believe one half I say. Still, I *am* innocent, and I will make a clean breast if I die for it."

What he stated was in substance as follows: He had lately made a voyage to the Indian Archipelago.[1] A group of people he joined had landed at Borneo and passed into the interior on a pleasure trip. He and a companion had captured the Ourang-Outang. This companion having died, the animal fell entirely into his possession. After great trouble caused by the fierceness

[1] Indian Archipelago—the islands of the Indian Ocean.

of the beast on the homeward journey, he had lodged it in his own home in Paris, where he had kept it carefully hidden until it had recovered from a wound in its foot, received from a splinter on board ship. His plan was to sell it.

Returning home from a party in the early morning in question, he had found the beast occupying his own bedroom, into which it had broken from a nearby closet, where it had been, as he thought, securely confined. Razor in hand and fully lathered, it was sitting before a mirror, attempting the operation of shaving, in which it had no doubt previously watched its master through the keyhole of the closet. Terrified at the sight of so dangerous a weapon in the possession of an animal so ferocious and so well able to use it, the man was at a loss what to do. He had been accustomed, however, to quiet the creature, even in its fiercest moods, by the use of a whip, and this he now seized. At sight of it, the Ourang-Outang sprang at once through the door of the room, down the stairs, and through an open window into the street.

The Frenchman followed in despair. The ape, razor in hand, occasionally looked back and gestured at its pursuer until the latter had nearly come up with it. It then again made off. In this manner the chase continued for a long time. The streets were completely quiet, as it was nearly three o'clock in the morning. In passing down an alley in the rear of the Rue Morgue, the fugitive's attention was caught by a light gleaming from the window of Madame L'Espanaye's room in the fourth story of her house. Rushing to the building, it perceived the lightning rod, clambered up it with agility, grasped the shutter, which was thrown fully back against the wall, and by this means swung itself directly upon the headboard of the bed. The whole thing did not occupy a minute. The shutter was kicked open again by the beast as it entered the room.

The sailor, in the meantime, now had great hopes of recapturing the brute, as it was apparently caught in a trap. On the other hand, he was very anxious as to what it might do in the house. So he followed the fugitive. A sailor can climb a lightning rod without difficulty; but when he had arrived at the window, which lay far to his left, he was stopped; the most he could accomplish was to reach over so as to obtain a glimpse of the interior of the room. At the sight within he nearly fell from his perch in horror. It was at this time those hideous shrieks arose, which had startled from slumber the inhabitants of the Rue Morgue. Madame L'Espanaye and her daughter, dressed in their night clothes, had apparently been arranging some papers in the iron chest, already mentioned, which had been wheeled into the middle of the room. The victims must have been sitting with their backs toward the window; and, from the screams, it seems probable that they did not see the animal at once.

As the sailor looked in, the gigantic animal had seized Madame L'Espanaye by the hair and was flourishing the razor before her face in imitation of the motions of a barber. The daughter had fainted. The screams and struggles of the old lady, during which her hair was torn from her head, had the effect of changing the probably peaceful purpose of the Ourang-Outang to one of wrath. With one sweep of its muscular arm, it nearly separated her head from her body. The sight of blood inflamed its anger into frenzy. Gnashing its teeth and flashing fire from its eyes, it flew upon the girl and buried its fearful claws in her throat, keeping its hold until she died.

At this moment its wild glances fell upon the head of the bed, over which the face of its master, rigid with horror, could be seen. The fury of the beast, who no doubt still remembered the whip, was changed into fear. Conscious of having deserved punishment, it seemed anxious to conceal its bloody deeds and skipped about the chamber in an agony of nervous agitation—throwing down and breaking the furniture as it moved, and dragging the bed from the bedstead. At the end it seized first the corpse of the daughter, and thrust it up the chimney, as it was found, and then that of the old lady, which it immediately hurled through the window.

As the ape approached the window with its burden, the sailor clung terrified to the rod, and, rather gliding than climbing down it, hurried home, dreading the consequences of the butchery and gladly giving up, in his terror, all anxiety about the fate of the Ourang-Outang. The words heard by the party on the staircase were the Frenchman's exclamations of horror and fright mingled with the fiendish jabbering of the brute.

I have scarcely anything to add. The beast must have

escaped from the room by the rod just before the breaking down of the door. It must have closed the window as it passed through. It was later caught by the owner himself, who sold it for a very large sum to a zoo. Le Bon was instantly released after Dupin had related, with some comment, all the circumstances to the Prefect of Police. That dignitary, however friendly toward my companion, could not entirely conceal his chagrin at the turn of affairs and indulged in a sarcasm or two about everyone minding his own business.

"Let him talk," said Dupin later. "Let him talk. It will ease his conscience. I am satisfied with having beaten him at his own game. Nevertheless, it is no mystery that he failed in the solution of the crime. Our friend, the Prefect, is too *cunning* to be *profound*. But he is a good creature. I like him especially for one master stroke of pretense by which he has gained his reputation for cleverness. I mean the way he has of 'denying that which is and explaining that which is not'."

# THE PURLOINED LETTER

IN PARIS, just after dark one windy evening in the autumn, I was enjoying the double luxury of my thoughts and my pipe in company with my friend, C. Auguste Dupin, in his little library at No. 33 Rue Dunot, Faubourg St. Germain. For one hour at least we had maintained complete silence, while each of us might have seemed occupied only with the curling smoke that filled the room. I, however, was considering certain topics we had been discussing earlier in the evening—I mean, the affair of the Rue Morgue, which Dupin had solved. I considered it, then, something of a coincidence when the door of our apartment was thrown open to admit our old acquaintance, Monsieur G.——, the Prefect of the Paris police.

We gave him a hearty welcome, for he was an entertaining man, and we had not seen him for several years. We had been sitting in the dark, and Dupin now arose to light a lamp. He sat down again without doing so when he heard G. say that he had called to consult us, or rather to ask the opinion of my friend about some official business which had caused a great deal of trouble.

"If it is anything that requires thought," observed Dupin, "we shall deal with it better in the dark."

"That is another of your odd notions," said the Prefect, who considered everything odd that he could not understand, and so lived among a multitude of oddities.

"Very true," said Dupin, as he supplied his visitor with a pipe and rolled a comfortable chair toward him.

"And what is the difficulty now?" I asked. "Nothing more in the way of murder, I hope."

"Oh, no; nothing like that. The fact is, the business is very simple indeed, and I do not doubt that we can manage it sufficiently well ourselves; but then I thought Dupin would like to hear the details of it, because it is so exceedingly *odd.*"

"Simple and odd," said Dupin.

"Why, yes; and not exactly that either. The fact is, we have all been a good deal puzzled because the affair *is* so simple, and yet it baffles us altogether."

"Perhaps it is the very simplicity of the thing which leads you astray," said my friend.

"What nonsense you do talk," replied the Prefect, laughing heartily.

"Perhaps the mystery is a little *too* plain," said Dupin.

"Ha! Ha! Ha!" roared our visitor. "Oh, Dupin, you will be the death of me yet."

"And what, after all, is the matter on hand?" I asked.

"Why, I will tell you," replied the Prefect, as he gave a long steady puff on his pipe and settled himself in his chair. "I will tell you in a few words; but before I begin let me warn you that this is an affair demanding the greatest secrecy. I should probably lose my position if it were known that I had told anyone about it."

"Proceed," said I.

"Or don't," said Dupin.

"Well then, I have received personal information from a very high quarter that a certain document of the highest importance has been stolen from the royal residence. The person who stole it is known; he was seen to take it. It is known, also, that it still remains in his possession."

"How is this known?" asked Dupin.

"Because of the nature of the document," replied the Prefect, "and because there would have been certain results if it had passed out of the robber's possession. We would know if he had used it as he must intend in the end to use it."

"Be a little clearer," I said.

"Well, I may venture to say that the paper gives its holder a certain power where power is immensely valuable."

"Still, I do not quite understand," said Dupin.

"No? Well, if a third person, whom I shall not name, should know about the document, the honor of a very important person would be damaged. This gives the man who holds the paper considerable power over the important person."

"But this power," I interrupted, "would depend on the loser's knowing who had robbed him. Who would dare . . . ?"

"The thief," said G., "is the Minister D., who dares all things. The method of the theft was clever as well as bold. The document in question—a letter, to be frank—had been received by the person robbed while she was alone in the royal boudoir. While she was reading it, she was suddenly interrupted by the entrance of the person from whom she especially wanted to hide it. After a hurried and vain attempt to put it in a drawer, she was forced to place it, open as it was, upon a table. The address, however, was uppermost. At this point the Minister D. enters. His keen eye immediately sees the paper, recognizes the handwriting of the address, observes the confusion of the owner of the letter, and figures out her secret. After some business transaction, hurried through in his ordinary manner, he produces a letter somewhat similar to the one in question, opens it, pretends to read it, and then places it close to the other. Again he talks for some fifteen minutes about public affairs. At length, in taking leave, he helps himself to the letter to which he had no claim. Its rightful owner saw but dared not call attention to the act in presence of the third person, who stood at her elbow. The Minister departed, leaving his letter of no importance on the table."

"So then," said Dupin to me, "you have what is needed to make the power complete. The robber knows the loser knows he has the letter."

"Yes," replied the Prefect, "and the robber has for some months used his power for political purposes to a very dangerous extent. The person robbed is more thoroughly convinced every day of the necessity of getting her letter back. But this, of course, cannot be done openly. Driven to despair, she has called in my aid."

"It is clear," said I, "as you observe, that the letter is still in the possession of the Minister. Only so long as he holds the letter can he have the power over his victim."

"True," said G. "And upon this knowledge I proceeded. My first task was to make a thorough search of the Minister's palace. Here my chief difficulty lay in the necessity of searching without his knowledge. Beyond all things I have been warned of the danger which would result from giving him reason to suspect our purpose."

"But," said I, "you are quite experienced in these investigations. The Parisian police have done this thing often before."

"Oh, yes; and for that reason I did not despair. The habits of the Minister, too, gave me a great advantage. He is frequently absent from home all night. His servants are few. They sleep at a distance from their master's room. I have, you know, keys with which I can open any room or cabinet in Paris. For three months I have spent almost every night ransacking his house. To mention a great secret, the reward is enormous. So I did not give up the search until I had become entirely sure that the thief is a cleverer man than myself. I think that I have investigated every nook and corner of the premises in which it is possible that the paper can be hidden."

"But is it not possible," I suggested, "that although the letter may be in possession of the Minister, as it undoubtedly is, he may have concealed it elsewhere than in his own home?"

"This is scarcely possible," said Dupin. "The sort of plots with which D. is known to be connected would make it extremely important that he be able to produce the letter at a minute's notice."

"The paper, then," I observed, "is clearly on the premises. We may consider it out of the question that the Minister is carrying it on his person."

"Entirely," said the Prefect. "He has been twice held up, as if by highwaymen, and carefully searched under my own supervision."

"You might have spared yourself that trouble," said Dupin. "D. is not altogether a fool and might have anticipated that as a matter of course."

"Not altogether a fool," said G., "but then he is a poet, which I take to be pretty close to it."

"True," said Dupin, after a long and thoughtful whiff

on his pipe, "although I have been guilty of some doggerel myself."

"Suppose you give us the particulars of your search," said I.

"Why, the fact is, we took our time and searched everywhere. I have had much experience in these affairs. I took the entire building, room by room, devoting the nights of a whole week to each. We examined first the furniture of each room. We opened every possible drawer; and I presume you know that to a properly trained police agent such a thing as a 'secret' drawer is impossible. The thing is so plain. There is a certain amount of space to be accounted for in every cabinet. Then we have accurate rules. The fiftieth part of an inch could not escape us. After the cabinets we took the chairs. The cushions we probed with fine long needles. From the tables we removed the tops."

"Why so?"

"Sometimes the top of a table or other similarly arranged piece of furniture is removed by the person wishing to hide an article; then the leg is dug out, the article placed within the cavity, and the top replaced. The bottoms and tops of bedposts are used in the same way."

"But could not the cavity be discovered by tapping?"

"By no means, if, when the article is put in, a sufficient wadding of cotton is placed around it. Besides, in our case, we had to proceed without noise."

"But you could not have taken to pieces all articles of

furniture. A letter may be compressed into a thin, spiral roll, much like a large knitting needle in shape and bulk, and in this form might be put into the rung of a chair, for example. You did not take apart all the chairs?"

"Certainly not; but we did better—we examined the rung of every chair and the joints of every type of furniture by the aid of a most powerful microscope. If there had been any traces of recent disturbance, we should not have failed to find it instantly. A single grain of gimlet-dust, for example, would have been as obvious as an apple. Any marks in the gluing, any unusual gaps in the joints would have made detection sure."

"I presume you examined mirrors and probed the beds and the bedclothes as well as the curtains and carpets?"

"Of course; and when we had completed every bit of the furniture in this way, then we examined the house itself. We divided its entire surface into sections, which we numbered so that none might be missed; then we examined each square inch throughout the premises, including the two houses next door, with the microscope as before."

"The two houses next door!" I exclaimed; "you must have had a great deal of trouble."

"We had; but the reward offered is enormous."

"You include the grounds around the houses?"

"All the grounds are paved with brick. They gave us comparatively little trouble. We examined the moss between the bricks and found it undisturbed."

"You looked among D.'s papers, of course, and into the books in his library?"

"Certainly; we opened every package and parcel; we not only opened every book, but we turned over every leaf in each volume, not being satisfied with a mere shake, according to the fashion of some policemen. We also measured the thickness of every book *cover*, with the most accurate measure, and applied to each the most careful examination with the microscope. If any bindings had recently been meddled with, we would have known. Some five or six volumes just from the printer we carefully probed with needles."

"You explored the floors beneath the carpets?"

"Of course. We removed every carpet and examined the boards with the microscope."

"And the paper on the walls?"

"Yes."

"You looked into the cellars?"

"We did."

"Then," I said, "you have been making a mistake, and the letter is *not* on the premises, as you suppose."

"I fear you are right," said the Prefect. "And now, Dupin, what would you advise me to do?"

"To make a thorough search of the premises."

"That is absolutely needless," replied G. "I am not more sure that I breathe than I am that the letter is not at the house."

"I have no better advice to give you," said Dupin. "You have, of course, an accurate description of the letter?"

"Oh yes!"—And here the Prefect, producing a memorandum-book, proceeded to read aloud a minute description of the appearance of the missing document. Soon afterward he departed, more gloomy in spirits than I had ever known the good gentleman to be.

About a month afterward, he paid us another visit and found us occupied very nearly as before. He took a pipe and a chair and entered into some ordinary conversation. At length I said, "But, G., what of the purloined letter? I presume you have at last made up your mind that there is no such thing as outsmarting the Minister."

"Confound him, say I—yes. I made the re-examination as Dupin suggested, but it was all labor lost, however, as I knew it would be."

"How much was the reward offered, did you say?" said Dupin.

"Why, a great deal. I wouldn't mind giving my individual check for fifty thousand francs to anyone who could get me that letter. The fact is, it is becoming of more and more importance every day, and the reward has lately been doubled. If it were trebled, however, I could do no more than I have done."

"Why, yes," drawled Dupin between whiffs on his pipe, "I really think, G., you have not exerted yourself to the utmost in this matter. You might do a little more, I think."

"How? In what way?"

"Why, you might employ counsel in the matter, eh?"

"I am *perfectly* willing to take advice," said the Prefect, a little annoyed, "and to pay for it. I would *really* give fifty thousand francs to anyone who would aid me in the matter."

"In that case," said Dupin, opening a drawer and producing a checkbook, "you might as well write me a check for the amount mentioned. When you have signed it, I will hand you the letter."

I was astonished. The Prefect appeared absolutely thunder-struck. For some minutes he remained speechless and motionless. Then, apparently recovering himself in some measure, he seized a pen, signed a check for fifty thousand francs, and handed it across the table to Dupin. The latter examined it carefully and put it in his pocket book. Then, unlocking a desk, he took from it a letter and gave it to the Prefect, who grasped it in a perfect agony of joy. He opened it with trembling hands, cast a rapid glance at its contents, and then rushed from the house without having uttered a syllable since Dupin had requested him to write the check.

When he had gone, my friend entered into some explanations. "The Parisian police," he said, "are exceedingly able in their way. They are persevering, clever, and thoroughly trained in the knowledge which their duties demand. When G. told us his method of searching the Minister's premises, I felt entire confidence in his having made a satisfactory investigation—so far as his labors extended. The measures adopted were not only the best of their kind, but carried out to absolute perfection. Had the letter been placed within range of their search, these fellows would, beyond question, have found it."

I merely laughed, but he seemed quite serious. "The measures, then," he continued, "were good in their kind. They just didn't apply to the case and to the man. The Prefect has a set of clever methods which he uses in all cases. But he perpetually makes mistakes by being either too deep or too shallow for the matter in hand; and many a school boy is a better reasoner than he."

"In other words," I said, "he should be able to measure his opponent's intellect with his and then choose his method of search."

"The Prefect and his followers fail so frequently because they consider only their *own* ideas of cleverness; and in searching for anything hidden consider only the methods by which *they* would have hidden it.

"Consider the case of the Prefect. What does all his boring and probing and examining with the microscope mean? Do you not see that he has taken it for granted that *all* men try to hide a letter in *some* out-of-the-way hole or corner? Do you not also see that such places of concealment are used only under ordinary circumstances and by ordinary people? Then the discovery of the article stolen depends only on the patience and determination of the seekers and not at all on their cleverness. And where the case is important or the reward is great, the usual methods have never been known to fail.

"Now you will understand what I meant in suggesting that if the letter had been hidden anywhere within the boundaries of the Prefect's search, its discovery would have been certain. That official, however, has been thoroughly bewildered—because he supposes that the Minister is a fool. He is famed as a poet; all fools are poets. This the Prefect feels, just as he thence concludes that all poets are fools."

"But is this really the poet?" I asked. "There are two brothers, I know, and both are noted for their writings. The Minister, I believe, has written learnedly on advanced mathematics. He is a mathematician and no poet."

"You are mistaken. I know him well. He is both. As mathematician he would not have reasoned at all and thus would have been at the mercy of the Prefect."

"You surprise me," I said. "Mathematical reasoning has always been considered the best in the world."

"I dispute," said Dupin, "the value of the sort of reasoning that the science of mathematics develops. Mathematical reasoning applies only to the observation of *forms* and *quantities*. It does not apply to the abstract or general truths about life or human beings. If the Minister had been only a mathematician, the Prefect would not have lost his reward money. I knew him as a courtier, too, and as a bold schemer. Such a man, I considered, could not fail to know that he would be waylaid. He must have foreseen, I figured, the secret searches of his house. His frequent absences from home I regarded only as tricks to give the police opportunity for a thorough search and then to impress them with the idea—which G. actually did get—that the letter was not there.

"I felt also," continued Dupin, "that the Minister would thus despise all ordinary places of concealment. He could not, I figured, be so dull as not to see that the most hidden places of his home would be as open to the inspection of the Prefect as his most open closets. I saw, in short, that he would be driven to the use of a very simple place. You will remember, perhaps, how heartily the Prefect laughed when I suggested that it was possible that the mystery troubled him so much on account of its being so *very* plain."

"Yes," I said, "I remember his merriment well. I really thought he would have a convulsion."

"There is a game of puzzles," said Dupin, "which is played upon a map. One party playing requires another to find a given word—the name of a town or a river, a state or an empire. A beginner in the game generally tries to puzzle his opponents by giving them a word with the smallest letters on the map. But the expert selects such words as stretch in large letters from one end of the map to the other. These escape notice merely by being too noticeable. This is a point, it seems, above or beneath the understanding of the Prefect. He never thought it once possible that the Minister had deposited the letter immediately beneath the nose of the whole world, by way of best preventing any part of the world from seeing it.

"The more I thought about the daring and cleverness of the Minister, about the fact that the letter had to be always at hand if he meant to use it, and about the evidence secured by the Prefect that it was not hidden where the police could find it, the more sure I became that to hide the letter, the Minister had used the trick of not trying to hide it at all.

"Full of these ideas, I equipped myself with a pair of strong dark glasses and called one fine morning, quite by accident, at the Minister's home. I found him there lounging about as usual and pretending to be filled with boredom. He is possibly the most really energetic human being alive, but that is only when nobody sees him.

"To be even with him, I complained of my weak eyes and regretted my need of spectacles—which made it possible for me to examine the whole place cautiously but thoroughly, while seeming to be interested only in the conversation of my host.

"I paid special attention to a large desk near which he sat and upon which lay in confusion letters, papers, one or two musical instruments, and a few books. Here, however, I saw nothing to arouse any particular suspicion.

"At length my eyes fell upon a cheap card rack of paste-board which hung dangling by a dirty blue ribbon from a little brass knob just below the middle of the mantel-piece. In this rack, which had three or four compartments, were five or six visiting cards and one letter. This last was very much soiled and crumpled. It was torn nearly in two across the middle, as if some one had first planned to tear it up as worthless and then had changed his mind. It had a large black seal bearing the Minister's coat of arms and was addressed in a small feminine hand to the Minister himself. It was thrust carelessly into one of the divisions of the rack.

"No sooner had I glanced at this letter than I concluded it was the one I wanted. To be sure, it was to all appearances entirely different from the one of which the Prefect had read us such a careful description. The size alone was similar. But then, the soiled and torn paper was so unlike the methodical habits of D. and so plainly a scheme to make a searcher believe the document was worthless. These things, together with the too noticeable position of the paper, in the full view of every visitor, exactly as I had previously concluded it would be, made me very suspicious of it.

"I lengthened my visit as much as possible, and while I held a lively discussion with the Minister, I kept my attention fixed upon the letter. In this examination I memorized its appearance and the arrangement in the rack and also, at the last, discovered something which set at rest any doubts I might have had. In gazing at the edges of the paper, I saw that they had a broken appearance, such as one sees when a stiff paper, having been once folded and pressed, is refolded in the opposite direction, in the same creases or edges which had formed the original fold. It was clear to me that the letter had been turned, like a glove, inside out, redirected, and resealed. I bade the Minister good morning and took my departure at once, leaving a gold snuff-box on the table.

"The next morning I called for the snuff-box, and we continued eagerly the conversation of the preceding day. While we were thus occupied, however, a loud report as of a pistol was heard beneath the windows of the house. This was followed by a series of fearful screams and the shoutings of a terrified mob. D. rushed to the window, opened it, and looked out. In the meantime I stepped to the card rack, took the letter, put it in my pocket, and replaced it with a facsimile which I had carefully prepared here, imitating the D. seal.

"The disturbance in the street had been caused by the frantic behavior of a man with a musket. He had fired it among a crowd of women and children. It proved, however, to be unloaded, and the fellow turned out to be a lunatic or a drunkard. When he had gone, D. came from the window, to which I had followed him as soon as I had secured the letter. Soon afterward I bade him farewell. The pretended lunatic was a man I had hired."

"But what purpose had you," I asked, "in replacing the letter with a facsimile? Would it not have been better, at the first visit, to have seized it openly and departed?"

"D.," replied Dupin, "is a desperate man and a man of courage. If I had made the wild attempt you suggest, I might never have left the place alive. But I had another reason. You know my political ideas. In this matter I was on the side of the lady concerned. For eighteen months the Minister had her in his power. She now has him in hers, since, unaware that he no longer has the letter, he will go on with his demand as if he had. Thus he will bring about his own political destruction. His downfall, too, will be as fast as it is awkward. I have no sympathy for him. He is a man without principle. I must confess, though, that I would like to know how he feels when, the lady having at last defied him, he opens the letter which I left for him in the card-rack."

"Why? Did you put anything particular in it?"

"D. once did me an evil turn in Vienna, which I told him, quite good-humoredly, I should remember. So, as I knew he would feel some curiosity about the identity of the person who had outwitted him, I thought it a pity not to give him a clue. He is well acquainted with my special writing paper, and I just wrote in the middle of the blank sheet the words, 'A man is never so clever that he can't be outwitted by some one as clever as he.' "

# *Murder for Murder's Sake*

# THE TELL-TALE HEART

TRUE!—very, very dreadfully nervous I have been and am. But why *will* you say that I am mad? The disease I suffered from had sharpened my senses, not destroyed, not dulled them. Above all, my sense of hearing was acute. I heard all things in heaven and earth. I heard many things in hell. How, then, could I be mad? Hearken! and observe how normally, how calmly I can tell you the whole story of what happened.

I cannot say how the idea first entered my brain; but, once there, it haunted me day and night. I had no motive for what I did; nor was I moved by any strong feeling. I loved the old man. He had never wronged me. He had never insulted me. I had no desire for his gold. I think it was his eye! Yes, that was it. One of his eyes resembled that of a vulture. It was a pale blue eye, with a film over it. Whenever it fell upon me, my blood ran cold; and so by degrees—very gradually—I made up my mind to take the life of the old man, and thus rid myself of the eye forever.

Now this is the point. You think me mad. Madmen know nothing. But you should have seen *me*. You should have seen how wisely I proceeded—with what caution, with what foresight, with what craft I went to work. I was never kinder to the old man than during the whole week before I killed him.

Every night, about midnight, I turned the latch of his door and opened it—oh, so gently! Then, when I had made an opening sufficient for my head, I put in a dark lantern, all closed, so that no light shone out. Then I thrust in my head. Oh, you would have laughed to see how cleverly I thrust it in. I moved it slowly—very, very slowly, so that I would not disturb the old man's sleep. It took me an hour to place my whole head within the opening far enough to see him as he lay upon his bed. Ha! Would a madman have been so wise as this?

Then, when my head was well in the room, I opened the lantern cautiously—oh so cautiously (for the hinges creaked). I uncovered it just enough for a single thin ray of light to fall upon the vulture eye.

And this I did for seven long nights, every night just at midnight, but I found the eye always closed, and so it was impossible to do the work. It was not the old man who vexed me, but his Evil Eye. And every morning, when the day came, I went boldly into his room and spoke courageously to him, calling him by name in a hearty tone and inquiring how he had passed the night. So you see he would have been a very wise old man indeed to suspect that every night, just at twelve, I looked in upon him while he slept.

Upon the eighth night I was more than usually cautious in opening the door. A watch's minute hand moves more quickly than did mine. Never before that night had I felt the extent of my own powers—of my keenness. I could scarcely contain my feelings of triumph to think that there I was, opening the door, little by little, without his even dreaming of my secret deeds or thoughts. I fairly chuckled at the idea; and perhaps he heard me, for he moved on the bed suddenly, as if startled. Now you may think that I drew back—but no. His room was as black as pitch with the thick darkness, and so I knew he could not see the opening of the door. I kept on pushing it, steadily, steadily.

I had my head in and was about to open the lantern when my thumb slipped upon the fastening, and the old man sprang up in bed, crying out, "Who's there?"

I kept quite still and said nothing. For a whole hour I did not move a muscle, and in the meantime I did not hear him lie down. He was still sitting up in the bed listening, just as I had done, night after night, haunted by evil thoughts.

Presently I heard a slight groan, and I knew it was the groan of mortal terror. It was not a groan of pain or of grief. It was the low, stifled sound that arises from the depth of a terrified soul. I knew the sound well.

Many a night, just at midnight, when all the world slept, it has welled up from my own heart, deepening, with its dreadful echo, the terrors that distracted me.

I knew what the old man felt and pitied him, though I chuckled at heart. I knew that he had been lying awake ever since the first slight noise when he had turned in bed. His fears had been ever since growing upon him. He had been trying to imagine them causeless, but could not. He had been saying to himself, "It is nothing but the wind in the chimney. It is only a mouse crossing the floor." Yes, he had been trying to comfort himself with these assurances; but all in vain. *All in vain;* because Death, in approaching him, had stalked with his black shadow before him and enveloped the victim. It was the horrible influence of this unseen shadow that caused him to *feel*—although he neither saw nor heard—the presence of my head within the room.

When I had waited a long time, very patiently, without hearing him lie down, I resolved to open a little, a very, very little crack in the lantern. So I opened it—you cannot imagine how stealthily—until at length a single dim ray, like the thread of the spider, shone full upon the vulture eye.

It was open—wide, wide open—and I grew furious as I gazed upon it. I saw it with perfect distinctness—all a dull blue, with a hideous veil over it that chilled the very marrow in my bones. I could see nothing else of the old man's face or person, for I had directed the ray as if by instinct precisely upon the damned spot.

And now—have I not told you that what you mistake for madness is but over-keenness of the senses? Now, I say, there came to my ears a low, dull, quick sound, such as a watch makes when wrapped in cotton. I knew *that* sound well, too. It was the beating of the old man's heart. It increased my fury as the beating of a drum stimulates the soldier into courage.

But even yet I kept still. I scarcely breathed. I held the lantern motionless. I tried to see how steadily I could keep the ray upon the eye. Meanwhile, the hellish tattoo of the heart increased. It grew quicker and quicker and louder and louder every instant. The old man's terror must have been awful. It grew louder, I say, louder every moment. I have told you that I am nervous. So I am. Now at the dead hour of the night, amid the dreadful silence of that old house, so strange a noise as this excited me to uncontrollable terror.

For some minutes longer I stood still. But the beating grew louder, louder! I thought the heart must burst. And now a new anxiety seized me—the sound would be heard by a neighbor! The old man's hour had come. With a loud yell I threw open the lantern and leaped into the room. He shrieked only once. In an instant I dragged him to the floor and pulled the heavy mattress over him. I smiled gaily to find the deed so far done.

But for many minutes the heart beat on with a muffled sound. This, however, did not disturb me; it would not be heard through the wall. At length it ceased. The old man was dead. I removed the mattress and examined the corpse. Yes, he was dead, stone dead.

I placed my hand upon his heart and held it there many minutes. There was no pulsation. He was stone dead. His eye would trouble me no more.

If you still think me mad, you will do so no longer when I describe the wise precautions I took for the concealment of the body. The night passed, and I worked hastily, but in silence. First of all, I dismembered the corpse. I cut off the head and the arms and the legs.

I took up three planks from the flooring of the chamber and deposited all between the beams. I then replaced the boards so cleverly that no human eye, not even *his*, could have detected anything wrong. There was nothing to wash out—no stains of any kind, no blood-stain whatever. I had been too careful for that. A tub had caught all—ha! ha!

When I had made an end of these labors, it was four o'clock—still dark as midnight. As the clock struck the hour, there came a knocking at the street door. I went down to open it with a light heart—for what had I *now* to fear? There entered three men, who introduced themselves with perfect courtesy as officers of the police. A shriek had been heard by a neighbor during the night. Suspicion of foul play had been aroused. Information had been lodged at the police office, and they had been deputed to search the premises.

I smiled—for what had I to fear? I bade the gentlemen welcome. The shriek, I said, was my own in a dream. The old man, I mentioned, was away in the country. I took my visitors all over the house. I bade them search—search well. I led them at length to *his* room. I showed them his treasures, secure, undisturbed. In the enthusiasm of my confidence, I brought chairs into the room and invited them to rest there from their weariness, while I myself in the wild confidence of my perfect triumph placed my own chair upon the very spot beneath which lay the corpse of the victim.

The officers were satisfied. My *manner* had convinced them. I was singularly at ease. They sat, and while I answered cheerily, they chatted of familiar things. But, ere long, I felt myself growing pale and wished them gone. My head ached, and I fancied a ringing in my ears. But still they sat and still chatted. The ringing continued and became more distinct. I talked more freely to get rid of the feeling, but it continued and gained clearness—until, at length, I found that the noise was *not* within my ears!

No doubt I now grew very pale—but I talked more fluently and with a louder voice. Yet the sound increased—and what could I do? It was *a low, dull, quick sound—much such a sound as a watch makes when wrapped in cotton.* I gasped for breath. The officers had apparently not heard it. I talked more quickly, more excitedly; but the noise steadily increased. I stood up and argued about trifles in a high key with violent motions, but the noise steadily increased. Why *would* they not go?

I paced the floor with heavy strides as if excited to fury—but the noise steadily increased. Oh God! What *could* I do. I foamed, I raved, I swore. I swung the chair upon which I had been sitting and scraped it upon the floor, but the noise could be heard above all, and steadily increased. It grew louder, louder, *louder*. And still the men chatted pleasantly and smiled. Was it possible they did not hear? No! They heard, they suspected, they *knew*. They were making a mockery of my horror. This I thought, and this I think. But anything was better than this agony. Anything was more bearable than this scorn. I could bear those hypocritical smiles no longer. I felt that I must scream or die. And now again—listen—louder, louder, *louder!*

"Villains!" I shrieked, "mock me no more. I admit the deed. Tear it up—the plank!—here, here!—it is the beating of his hideous heart."

# THE BLACK CAT

FOR the wild narrative which I am about to write I neither expect nor request belief. I would be mad indeed to expect it in a case where I myself can scarcely believe what my own senses have proved to me. Yet I am not mad, and very surely I am not dreaming. Tomorrow I am going to die, and today I want to unburden my soul. My immediate purpose is to place before the world, plainly, briefly, and without comment, a series of mere household events. In their consequences these events have terrified—have tortured—have destroyed me. Yet I will not attempt to explain them. To me they have presented only horror. Hereafter, perhaps some wise man, more calm and more logical than I, will be found who will be able to see, in the circumstances I am about to relate, nothing more than an ordinary succession of very natural causes and effects.

From my infancy I was noted for the gentleness and kindness of my disposition. My heart was even so tender as to make me the jest of my companions. I was especially fond of animals and was allowed by my parents to have a great variety of pets. With these I spent most of my time and was never so happy as when feeding and fondling them. This characteristic of my nature continued as I grew older, and in my manhood I derived from it one of my principal sources of pleasure. I need not explain to those who have loved a wise and faithful dog the nature and strength of the satisfaction thus gained. There is something in the unselfish love of an animal which goes directly to the heart.

I married young and was happy to find in my wife a disposition congenial with my own. Observing my partiality for domestic pets, she lost no opportunity of procuring some. We had birds, gold-fish, a fine dog, rabbits, a small monkey, and a *cat*.

This latter was a remarkably large and beautiful animal, entirely black, and smart to an astonishing degree. In speaking of his intelligence, my wife, who was at heart a bit superstitious, made frequent reference to the ancient popular notion that all black cats are witches in disguise. Not that she was ever really serious about it.

Pluto—that was the cat's name—was my favorite pet and playmate. I alone fed him, and he followed me wherever I went about the house. It was even with difficulty that I prevented him from following me through the streets.

Our friendship lasted in this manner for several years. During this time, I am ashamed to confess, my own character made a radical change for the worse. As a result of constant drunkenness I grew, day by day, more moody, more irritable, and more indifferent to the feelings of others. I allowed myself to use harsh language to my wife. At length I even offered her personal violence. My pets, of course, were made to feel the change in my disposition. I not only neglected, but ill-used them. However, I still refrained from treating Pluto cruelly, as I did the rabbits, the monkey, or even the dog, when by accident or through affection they came my way. But my disease grew upon me—for what disease is like Alcohol? At length even Pluto, who was now becoming old and consequently somewhat peevish—even Pluto began to experience the effects of my ill temper.

One night, returning home, much intoxicated, from one of my haunts about town, I fancied that the cat avoided me. I seized him; in his fright at my violence he inflicted a slight wound upon my hand with his teeth. The fury of a demon instantly possessed me. I scarcely knew myself. My original self seemed to leave me, and a fiendish, gin-nurtured hatred seized me. I took from my pocket a penknife, opened it, grasped the poor beast by the throat, and deliberately cut one of its eyes from the socket. I shudder as I write this terrible atrocity.

When reason returned in the morning, and I had slept off the effects of the night's dissipation, I experienced a feeling half of horror, half of remorse, for the crime of which I had been guilty. It was not a very lasting feeling, however, and I again plunged into excesses and drowned in wine all memory of the deed.

In the meantime the cat slowly recovered. The socket of the lost eye presented, it is true, a frightful appearance, but the animal no longer appeared to suffer any pain. He went about the house as usual, but, as might be expected, fled in extreme terror at my approach. I had enough of my old nature left to be grieved by this evident dislike on the part of a creature that had once loved me so much; but this feeling soon gave place to irritation.

And then came, as a prelude to my final ruin, a spirit of contrariness on my part. Who has not a hundred times found himself committing a bad or a stupid action just because he knows he shouldn't? Haven't we all at some times a desire to violate a law just because we know it *is* a law? This urge contributed now to my final overthrow by making me continue and finally complete the injury I had inflicted on the harmless animal. One morning, in cold blood, I slipped a noose about its neck and hung it to the limb of a tree—hung it with tears streaming from my eyes and with the bitterest remorse in my heart. This I did *because* I knew that it loved me and *because* I felt it had given me no reason for anger. I realized that in so doing I was committing a mortal sin, which would endanger my immortal soul.

On the night of the day on which this cruel deed was done, I was aroused from sleep by the cry of fire. The curtains of my bed were in flames. The whole house was blazing. It was with great difficulty that my wife, a servant, and I made our escape. The destruction was complete. My entire worldly wealth was swallowed up, and I resigned myself thereafter to despair.

It is not my purpose to find a close connection between the disaster and the atrocity; but I am relating a chain of facts and do not wish to leave even a possible link imperfect. On the day after the fire, I visited the ruins. The walls, with one exception, had fallen in. This exception was a wall not very thick, which stood about the middle of the house and against which had rested the head of my bed. The plastering had here in great measure resisted the action of the fire, possibly because the wall there had been recently repaired, and the plaster was consequently rather new. Around this wall a huge crowd had collected, and many persons seemed to be examining a particular portion of it with eager attention. The words "strange," "remarkable," and other similar expressions excited my curiosity. I approached and saw, as if engraved upon the white surface, the figure of a gigantic *cat*. The impression was given with a truly marvelous accuracy. There was a rope around the animal's neck.

When I first beheld this, my wonder and terror were extreme; but at length reason came to my aid. The cat, I remembered, had been hung in a garden next to the house. Upon the alarm of fire this garden had been immediately filled by the crowd. Someone must have cut the animal down from the tree and thrown it, through an open window, into my room. This had probably been done to arouse me from sleep. The falling of other walls had compressed the victim of my cruelty into the substance of the freshly-spread plaster; the lime, with the flames, and the ammonia from the carcass, had then created the portraiture as I saw it.

This startling circumstance made a deep impression on my imagination. For months I could not rid myself of the picture of the cat; and during this period there came back to me a feeling that seemed like, but was not really, remorse. I went so far as to regret the loss of the animal and to look about me among my vile haunts for another pet of the same sort and of somewhat similar appearance to take its place.

One night as I sat, half stupefied, in a disreputable den, my attention was drawn to a black object, lying upon one of the huge casks of rum, which made up the chief furniture of the room. I had been looking steadily at the top of this cask for some minutes and was surprised that I had not sooner seen the object on it. It was a black cat—a very large one—fully as large as Pluto, and closely resembling him in every respect but one. Pluto had not a white hair on any portion of his body; but this cat had a large splotch of white of indefinite shape covering nearly all of its breast.

When I touched him, he immediately rose, purred loudly, rubbed against my hand, and appeared delighted at my notice. This, then, was the very creature

I was seeking. I at once offered to purchase it from the landlord; but he made no claim to it—knew nothing of it—had never seen it before. I continued my caresses, and when I prepared to go home, the animal showed a desire to accompany me. I allowed it to do so, occasionally stooping and patting it as I proceeded. When it reached the house, it settled down at once and immediately became a great favorite with my wife.

For my own part, I soon began to feel a dislike for it. This was just the opposite of what I had expected; but, I know not how or why, its evident fondness for me rather disgusted and annoyed me. By slow degrees these feelings increased into hatred. I avoided the creature; a certain sense of shame and the remembrance of my former deed of cruelty prevented me from physically abusing it. I did not, for some weeks, strike or otherwise ill-use it; but gradually, very gradually I came to look upon it with unutterable loathing and to flee from its presence. What added, no doubt, to my hatred of the beast was the discovery, the morning after I brought it home, that, like Pluto, it also had been deprived of one of its eyes. This, however, only endeared it to my wife, who, as I have already said, possessed to a high degree that kindness of feeling which had once been my strongest trait and the source of many of my simplest and purest pleasures.

With my dislike of this cat, however, its liking for me increased. It dogged my footsteps with a persistence which it would be hard to make the reader understand. Whenever I sat down, it would crouch beneath my chair or spring upon my knee, covering me with its loathsome caresses. If I arose to walk, it would get between my feet and thus nearly throw me down, or it would fasten its long sharp claws in my trousers and clamber up to my breast. At such times, although I longed to destroy it with a blow, I was withheld from doing so, partly by a memory of my former crime, but chiefly—let me confess it at once—by absolute *dread* of the beast.

This dread was not exactly a fear of physical evil, and yet I should be at a loss to explain it otherwise. Even in this criminal's cell I am ashamed to admit that the terror with which the animal filled me had been increased by a wild fancy of my imagination. My wife had called my attention more than once to the shape of the mark of white hair of which I have spoken, and which was the sole visible difference between this beast and the one I had destroyed. The reader will remember that this mark, although large, had originally been indefinite in form. By slow degrees—degrees almost imperceptible—and which my reason rejected as impossible, it had at length assumed a distinctness of outline. It had now the shape of an object I hesitate to name. For this above all I loathed and dreaded the monster and would have rid myself of him *had I dared.* It was now, I say, the image of a hideous, a ghastly thing—of the *gallows,* of that terrible engine of Horror and of Crime, of Agony and of Death!

And now I was wretched beyond belief. Neither by day nor by night did I know any more the blessing of rest. During the former, the creature left me no moment alone, and in the latter I started hourly from dreams of fear to find the hot breath of the thing upon my face and its vast weight, a nightmare that I had no power to shake off, lying upon my heart.

Under the pressure of torments such as these, the feeble remnant of the good within me died. Dark and evil thoughts became my sole companions. The moodiness of my usual temper increased to hatred of all things and all men. My uncomplaining wife was, alas, the usual patient sufferer from my sudden and frequent outbursts of fury.

One day she accompanied me upon some household errand into the cellar of the old building in which our poverty compelled us to live. The cat followed me down the steep stairs and, nearly throwing me headlong, exasperated me to madness. Lifting an axe and forgetting in my wrath the childish dread which had hitherto held me back, I aimed a blow at the animal, which, of course, would have proved instantly fatal had it descended as I intended. But this blow was arrested by the hand of my wife. Goaded by her interference into a rage more than insane, I withdrew my arm from her grasp and buried the axe in her brain. She fell dead upon the spot without a groan.

This hideous murder done, I set myself at once and with great deliberation to the task of concealing the body. I knew that I could not remove it from the house either by day or by night without the risk of being observed by the neighbors. Many ideas entered my mind. At one time I thought of cutting the corpse into minute fragments and destroying them by fire. At another I resolved to dig a grave for it in the floor of the cellar. Again I considered casting it in a well in the yard, or packing it in a box as though it were merchandise and having an expressman take it from the house. Finally I hit upon a far better plan than any of these. I determined to wall it up in the cellar as the monks in the Middle Ages are recorded to have walled up their victims.

For a purpose such as this the cellar was especially adapted. Its walls were loosely constructed and had lately been plastered throughout with a rough plaster, which the dampness of the atmosphere had prevented from hardening. Moreover, in one wall was a projection, caused by a false chimney, or fireplace, that had been filled up and made to resemble the rest of the cellar. I was sure that I could easily remove the bricks at this point, insert the corpse, and wall the whole thing up as before, so that no eye could detect anything suspicious.

In this calculation I was not deceived. By means of a crowbar I easily dislodged the bricks. Having carefully deposited the body against the inner wall, I propped it in that position. Then with little trouble I replaced the whole structure as it originally stood. Having previously procured the necessary materials, I prepared a plaster which could not be distinguished from the old, and with this very carefully went over the new brickwork. When I had finished, I felt satisfied that all was right. The wall did not present the slightest appearance of having been disturbed. The rubbish on the floor I had picked up with the utmost care. I looked around triumphantly and said to myself, "Here at least, then, my labors have not been in vain."

My next step was to look for the beast which had been the cause of so much wretchedness; for I had at length firmly resolved to put it to death. If I had been able to find it at that moment, there could have been no doubt of its fate; but it appeared that the crafty animal had been alarmed at the violence of my anger and had temporarily disappeared. It is impossible to describe the deep, blissful sense of relief which the absence of the hated animal afforded me. It did not make its appearance during the night. Thus for one night at least since its introduction into the house, I soundly and peacefully slept—yes, *slept,* even with the burden of the murder on my soul.

The second and the third day passed, and still my tormentor did not come. Once again I breathed as a free man. The monster, in terror, had fled the place forever! I should see it no more! My happiness was complete! The guilt of my dark deed disturbed me but little. Some few inquiries had been made of me, but these I readily answered. Even a search had been started, but of course nothing was discovered. I looked upon my future safety as secure.

Upon the fourth day after the murder, a party of the police came very unexpectedly into the house and proceeded again to make thorough search of the premises. Secure, however, in the safety of my place of concealment, I felt no apprehension whatever. The officers made me accompany them in their search. They left no nook or corner unexplored. At length, for the third or fourth time, they descended into the cellar. I did not even quiver. My heart beat as calmly as that of one who sleeps in innocence. I walked from end to end of the cellar. I folded my arms upon my bosom and roamed easily to and fro. The police were thoroughly satisfied and prepared to depart. My glee was too strong to be restrained. I hurried to say at least one word by way of triumph and to render doubly sure their belief in my innocence.

"Gentlemen," I said at last, as the party ascended the steps, "I am delighted that I have allayed your suspicions. I wish you all health and a little more courtesy. By the way, gentlemen, this is a very well-constructed house. (In my strong desire to say something easily, I scarcely knew what I uttered.) I may say an *excellently* well-constructed house. These walls—are you going, gentlemen?—these walls are solidly put together." And here, through the mere frenzy of boldness, I rapped heavily with a cane which I held in my hand upon that very portion of the brick work behind which stood the corpse of my wife.

But may God shield and deliver me! No sooner had the sounds of my blows sunk into silence than I was answered by a voice from within the tomb—by a cry at first muffled and broken, like the sobbing of a child, and then quickly swelling into one long, loud, and continuous scream. It was utterly inhuman, a howl, a wailing shriek, half of horror and half of triumph.

Of my own thoughts I need not speak. Fainting, I staggered to the opposite wall. For one instant the party on the stairs remained motionless, filled with terror and awe. In the next a dozen stout arms were toiling at the wall. It fell bodily.

The corpse, already greatly decayed and clotted with blood, stood erect before the eyes of the spectators. Upon its head, with red extended mouth and solitary eye of fire, sat the hideous beast whose craft had led me into murder and whose informing voice had consigned me to the hangman. I had walled the monster up within the tomb.

# THE CASK OF AMONTILLADO

I HAD stood the thousand injuries of Fortunato as well as I could; but when he dared to insult me, I vowed revenge. You, who know me so well, will not suppose, however, that I uttered a threat. *At length* I would be avenged, though with no danger to myself. I must not only punish him but do so safely. And he must realize my responsibility for his punishment.

Neither by word nor deed had I given Fortunato cause to suspect my ill-will. I continued, as was my custom, to smile in his face—and he could not know that my smile *now* was at the thought of his future burial and my long-awaited revenge.

He had a weak point—this Fortunato—although in other ways he was a man to be respected and even feared. He prided himself on his knowledge of good wine. In this respect I did not differ from him greatly. I, too, was knowing in Italian vintages and bought largely whenever I could.

It was about dusk one evening, during the carnival season, that I met my friend. He greeted me with excessive warmth, for he had been drinking too much. He was dressed as a clown, in a many-colored striped suit. On his head was a cone-shaped cap, trimmed with bells. I was so pleased to see him that I thought I would never stop shaking his hand.

I said to him, "My dear Fortunato, I am lucky to meet you. How remarkably well you are looking today. I have received a cask of what is supposed to be Amontillado wine, though I have my doubts of it."

"What?" said he. "Amontillado? Impossible! Not in the midst of the carnival!"

"I had my doubts," I replied, "and I was silly enough to pay the full price without consulting you in the matter. You were not to be found, and I was afraid of losing a bargain."

"Amontillado!" he exclaimed.

"I have my doubts," I replied. "As you are busy, I am on my way to Luchesi. He will tell me—"

"Luchesi cannot tell Amontillado from Sherry."

"And yet some fools think that his taste is as good as your own."

"Come, let us go."

"Where?"

"To your wine vault."

"My friend, no. I will not impose on your good nature. I see you have an engagement. Luchesi–"

"I have no engagement. Come."

"My friend, no. I see you are suffering from a severe cold. The vaults are unbearably damp."

"Let us go, nevertheless. The cold is nothing. Amontillado! You have been imposed on. As for Luchesi, he cannot tell Sherry from Amontillado."

Speaking thus, Fortunato seized my arm. Putting on a mask of black silk and drawing a cloak closely about me, I let him hurry me to my palace.

There were no servants at home. They were all making merry at the carnival. I had told them I would not return until morning and had given them orders not to stir from the house. I knew that as soon as my back was turned they would all disappear immediately.

I took two torches from their holders and, giving one to Fortunato, led him through several suites of rooms to the archway that led to the vaults. I went down a long and winding staircase, asking him to be careful as he followed. We came at length to the end of the descent and stood upon the damp ground of the caverns.

The gait of my friend was unsteady, and the bells upon his cap jingled as he strode. "The cask," he said.

"It is farther on," I said. "How long have you had that cough?"

"Ugh! Ugh! Ugh!" Coughing thus my poor friend found it impossible to reply for many minutes. "It is nothing," he said at last.

"Come," I said with decision. "We will go back; your health is precious. You are rich, respected, admired, beloved. You are happy, as once I was. You are a man to be missed. For me it is no matter. We will go back; you will be ill, and I cannot be responsible. Besides, there is Luchesi—"

"Enough," he said. "The cough is a mere nothing; it will not kill me. I shall not die of a cough."

"True, true," I replied. "I had no intention of alarming you needlessly. A drink of this Medoc will protect us from the damp."

Here I knocked off the neck of a bottle which I took from its shelf. "Drink," I said, handing him the wine.

He raised it to his lips with a leer. He paused and nodded to me familiarly, while his bells jingled.

"I drink," he said, "to the dead that lie buried around us."

"And I to your long life."

He again took my arm and we proceeded.

"These vaults," he said, "are extensive."

"My family, the Montresors," I replied, "were great and numerous."

The wine sparkled in his eyes and the bells jingled. We had passed through walls of piled bones, with empty casks stacked here and there, into the inmost recesses of the vaults. I paused again, and this time I seized Fortunato by an arm above the elbow. "The dampness," I said. "See, it increases. We are below the river bed. Drops of moisture trickle among the bones.

Come, we will go back before it is too late. Your cough—"

"It is nothing," he said. "Let us go on. But first, another drink of the Medoc."

I handed him a flagon. He emptied it at once. His eyes flashed with a fierce light. He laughed and threw the bottle upward with a gesture I did not understand.

I looked at him in surprise.

"You do not comprehend?" he asked.

"Not I," I replied.

"Then you are not a mason."

"Yes, yes," I said.

"You? Impossible! A mason?"

"A mason," I replied.

"A sign," he said.

"It is this," I answered, producing a trowel from beneath the folds of my cloak.

"You are joking," he said, recoiling a few paces. "But let us proceed to the Amontillado."

I replaced the tool beneath my coat and again offered him my arm. He leaned upon it heavily. We continued our route in search of the Amontillado, descending to a deep crypt[1] in which the foulness of the air caused our torches to glow rather than to flame.

At the far end of this crypt was a much smaller one. On three sides its walls were lined with human bones, piled to the vaults overhead. On the fourth the bones had been thrown down and lay scattered upon the earth,

[1] Crypt—a burial vault.

forming at one point a mound of some size. Within this wall we perceived a hollow place about four feet in depth, three in width, and six or seven in height.

It was in vain that Fortunato, holding up his dull torch, endeavored to pry into the depth of this recess. The feeble light was not strong enough to illumine the interior.

"Proceed," I said. "The Amontillado is in there. As for Luchesi—"

"He is an ignoramus," interrupted my friend, as he stepped unsteadily forward, while I followed immediately at his heels. In an instant he had reached the end of the niche and was bewildered to find his progress thus halted. Jumping forward and seizing him, I chained him to the wall. In its surface were two iron staples. From one of these hung a short chain, from the other a padlock. Throwing the links about his waist, I secured it. He was too surprised to resist. Withdrawing the key, I stepped back.

"Pass your hand," I said, "over the wall. Indeed, it is *very* damp. Once more let me *implore* you to return. No? Then I must positively leave you. But I must first give you all the little attentions in my power."

"The Amontillado!" exclaimed my friend, not yet recovered from his astonishment.

"True," I replied, "the Amontillado."

As I said these words, I busied myself among the pile of bones of which I had before spoken. Throwing them aside, I soon uncovered a quantity of building stone and mortar. With these materials and with the aid of my trowel, I began vigorously to wall up the entrance of the niche.

I had scarcely finished the first layer of the masonry when I discovered that the intoxication of Fortunato had in great measure worn off. I heard a low moaning cry from the depth of the recess. It was *not* the cry of a drunken man. Then there was a long silence. I laid the second tier and the third and the fourth before I heard furious vibrations of the chain. The noise lasted for several minutes, during which, in order that I might listen to it with more satisfaction, I ceased my labors and sat down upon the bones. When at last the clanking stopped, I continued with the trowel and finished without interruption the fifth, the sixth, and the seventh tier. The wall was now nearly level with my breast. I again paused, and holding the torch over the mason work, threw a few feeble rays upon the figure within.

A succession of loud and shrill screams, bursting suddenly from the throat of the chained form, seemed to thrust me violently back. For a brief moment I hesitated. I trembled, thinking foolishly that in some way he could escape. Then I replied to the yells of the man within with even louder, even stronger ones of my own. Soon he grew still.

It was now midnight, and my task was drawing to a close. I had completed the eighth, the ninth, and the tenth tier. I had finished a portion of the eleventh and last; there remained but a single stone to be fitted and plastered in. I struggled with its weight. I placed it partially in its destined position.

But now there came from out the niche a low laugh that raised the hairs on my head. It was succeeded by a sad voice, which I had difficulty in recognizing as that of the noble Fortunato. The voice said, "Ha! Ha!—a very good joke indeed—an excellent jest. We will have many a good laugh about it at the palace—he! he! he!—over our wine!"

"The Amontillado!" I said.

"Ha! ha! ha!—yes, the Amontillado. But is it not getting late? Will they not be awaiting us at the palace, the lady Fortunato and the rest? Let us be gone."

"Yes," I said, "let us be gone."

"*For the love* of *God,* Montresor!"

"Yes," I said, "for the love of God."

But to these words I listened in vain for a reply. I grew impatient. I called aloud, "Fortunato!"

No answer.

I called again, "Fortunato!"

No answer still. I thrust a torch through the remaining space and looked within. There came forth in return only a jingling of the bells. My heart grew sick; it was the dampness of the vaults that made it so. I hastened to end my labor. I forced the last stone in its position. I plastered it up. Against the new masonry I replaced the old pile of bones. For a half century no mortal has disturbed them. *Rest in peace.*

# *Horror-Haunted Castles*

# LIGEIA

I CANNOT remember how, when, or even exactly where I first became acquainted with the Lady Ligeia. Long years have since passed, and my memory is feeble through much suffering. Or perhaps I cannot *now* bring these points to mind because, in truth, the character of my beloved, her great learning, her unusual yet calm beauty, and the thrilling effect of her musical voice made their way into my heart so gradually that I did not even note the passage of time. Yet I believe that I met her first in some large, ancient city near the Rhine.

I have surely heard her speak of her family, which must have been a very old one. Ligeia! Ligeia! Now that I am buried in the sort of studies which should make me forget the outside world, the sweet sound of her name alone can bring back to my mind a picture of her who lives no more. And now, while I write, a recollection comes to me that I have *never known* the last name of her who was my friend, my betrothed, the partner of my studies, and finally my wife. Was it a playful act on the part of Ligeia? Or was it a test of the strength of my affection that I should ask her no questions? Or was it a romantic whim of my own? I recall the fact itself only indistinctly. It is no wonder that I have entirely forgotten the circumstances connected with it.

There is one topic, however, on which my memory does not fail me. It is the beauty of Ligeia. She was tall, somewhat slender, and, in her last days, even thin. Her dignity, her quiet ease, and the lightness of her footfalls were beyond description. She came and went like a shadow. I never knew she had entered my study until I heard the music of her low, sweet voice. There was a quality of strangeness in her very loveliness. I would examine the lines of her high, pale forehead and find it faultless, the skin like pure ivory. Her hair was a glossy black, curling luxuriantly. The delicate outlines of her nose were perfect. Her sweet mouth, the dimples around it, the radiance of her smile were heavenly.

The eyes of my beloved were far larger than the ordinary ones, though it was only at intervals, in moments of intense excitement that this became more than slightly noticeable. They were the most brilliant black, with eyelashes of great length. The brows, slightly irregular in outline, were dark too. The strangeness which I found in her eyes was in their *expression*, however. For long hours have I thought of it. Through a whole midsummer night I have struggled to understand it. What was the meaning which lay behind those brilliant orbs?

It often happens in our efforts to recall something long forgotten that we find ourselves on the very point of remembering without being able, in the end, to remember. Thus often, as I gazed intently into Ligeia's eyes, have I felt approaching a full understanding of their expression, only to have it at length entirely depart. Strange, too, it was that I found in the commonest of objects a reflection of their beauty—in a stream of sparkling water, in a perfect rose, in the grace of a moth or a butterfly, in the exchanged glances of love and respect between two old, old people.

One phase of the character of Ligeia was the violence of her thought, feeling, and actions. Of all the women whom I have ever known, she, the outwardly calm, was inwardly a prey to the strongest emotions. Of such feelings I could form no estimate except by the expression of her eyes, by the magic melody of her low voice, and by the fierceness of her wild words, made doubly effective by the calmness of her speech.

I have spoken of the learning of Ligeia; it was immense, such as I have never known in women. Upon any learned subject I never found my wife to be lacking. Only lately have I realized the full extent of her knowledge. Then I did not realize that it was amazing, though I was enough aware of her superiority over me to let her guide me through the investigations with which I was busily occupied during the early years of our marriage. How vivid was the delight I felt as she bent over me in my studies and showed me stretching out before me the path of knowledge!

How violent then was my grief, after some years, when I had to give up all those expectations! Without Ligeia I was but a child groping in the night. Without the radiance of her eyes all things became dull. Ligeia grew ill. Her eyes blazed too brightly; her pale fingers took on the waxen hue of the grave. I saw that she must die, and I struggled desperately with the grim angel of death. And the struggles of my wife were, to my astonishment, even stronger than my own. There had been much in her nature to lead me to believe that, to her, death would come without terrors. But not so. Words cannot convey the fierceness with which she tried to live. I groaned in anguish at the sight. I would have soothed, I would have reasoned; but, in the strength of her desire for life, sympathy and reason alike were vain. Yet not until the last was her outward calmness shaken. Her voice grew more gentle—grew more low—but I cannot repeat the wild meaning of the quiet words she uttered.

That she loved me I should not have doubted; and I should have known that to a nature such as hers love is no ordinary emotion. But only in death was I fully impressed with the depth of her affection. For long hours, holding my hand, she would pour out to me a devotion that was almost worship. How had I deserved to be blessed with such a confession? How had I deserved to be cursed with the loss of my beloved in the hour when she had made me what I was? In Ligeia's love for me I understood her longing, so wildly and so violently, to hold the life which was now going so rapidly away.

At high noon before the night in which she died, she called me to her side and bade me recite certain verses she had composed not many days before. They told of the struggle of man against the conqueror death. "O God," shrieked Ligeia, leaping to her feet and holding up her arms to heaven, "Divine Father, shall this be always so? Can man, the conquered, be not even once the conqueror? Who knows the mystery and the force of the will? Man does not let himself die unless his will is too weak to conquer death."

And now, as if worn out with emotion, she let her white arms fall and returned to her bed of death. And as she breathed her last sighs, there came mingled with them a low murmur from her lips. I bent close to her and heard again the words, "Man does not let himself die unless his will is too weak to conquer death."

She died; and I, crushed into the very dust with sorrow, could no longer endure the loneliness of my dwelling in the dim and decaying city by the Rhine. I had no lack of what the world calls wealth. Ligeia had brought me far more than ordinarily falls to the lot of mortals. After a few months, therefore, of weary and aimless wandering, I purchased and put in some repair a castle in one of the wildest and most deserted sections of England. The gloomy and dreary grandeur of the building and the primitive character of the place suited my feelings of utter despair. Yet, although I had altered the outside of the decaying castle very little, I indulged, perhaps with a faint hope of relieving my sorrow, in a display of magnificence within. Even in my childhood I had acquired a taste for such follies, and now they came back to me in the insanity of my grief. The gorgeous and fantastic draperies, the Egyptian carvings, the elaborate furniture, the patterns of tufted gold in the carpets were all indications of my madness. I had meanwhile become a slave to opium, and all my days were colored by my dreams.

These I must not pause to tell. Let me speak only of one room, forever under a curse. Into it, in a moment when my mind was almost gone, I led as my bride—as the successor of the unforgotten Ligeia—the fair-haired and blue-eyed Lady Rowena Trevanion of Tremaine. There is no part of the bridal chamber which is not now right before my eyes. What was wrong with the proud family of the bride when, through thirst for gold, they let enter a room *so* bedecked a daughter so beloved? The room, which lay in a high tower of the castle, was a pentagon[1] in shape and of vast size. The entire southern side was one huge window, a single pane of unbroken glass from Venice, tinted a leaden hue, so that the rays of either the sun or moon, passing through it, fell with a ghastly light on the objects within. The ceil-

[1] Pentagon—a five-sided figure.

ing of dark oak was high, vaulted, and adorned with wild and grotesque patterns. From the center of it hung, by a single gold chain with long links, a censer[1] of the same metal, so constructed that there wound in and out of its designs a continual succession of many-colored fires.

About the room were couches and golden candelabra of Eastern design. The bridal bed was sculptured of solid ebony. In each of the angles of the room stood on end a giant coffin of black granite from the tombs of the kings of ancient Egypt. But the draping of the room was the most fantastic of all. The lofty walls were hung from ceiling to floor with a heavy tapestry. The same material covered the floor and couches and was used for the canopy of the bed and for the curtains which shaded the windows. The material was the richest cloth of gold, with designs worked in patterns of jet black—patterns which seemed to alter their forms as one approached them. To one just entering the room they were merely grotesque designs; but step by step, as the visitor moved about, they took on the forms of monsters and demons too terrible to describe. The whole effect was added to by a strong continual current of wind behind the draperies, which gave a hideous and uneasy life to everything.

In a castle such as this, in a bridal chamber such as this, I passed with the Lady of Tremaine the first month of our marriage. I could not help seeing that my wife dreaded the fierce moodiness of my temper, that she

[1] Censer—A vessel for perfume.

shunned me, and that she loved me but little. It rather gave me pleasure. I loathed her with a hatred belonging more to a demon than to a man. My memory flew back to Ligeia, the beloved, the beautiful, the dead. I thought longingly of her purity, her wisdom, her passionate love for me. My love for her burned madly. In the excitement of my opium dream I would call her name aloud in the silence of the night, or by day in the darkness of the forests where I roamed, as though by my longing for her I could restore her to life.

About the start of the second month of my marriage, the Lady Rowena was attacked with sudden illness, from which her recovery was slow. The fever with which she was burning made her nights uneasy. In her disturbed state of half-slumber, she spoke of sounds and motions in and about the tower room which I thought had no cause but her imagination, or perhaps the uncanny influence of the room itself. She became at last convalescent, and finally well. Yet only a brief period passed by before a second, more violent illness seized her. From this attack her constitution, at all times frail, never altogether recovered. Her illnesses were, after this period, of alarming nature and of more alarming frequency, defeating the knowledge and the great efforts of her doctors. With the increase of her chronic disease, apparently incurable by human means, I could not fail to observe a similar increase in the nervous irritation of her disposition and in her excitement over trifling causes of fear. She spoke again, now more frequently and persistently, of the slight sounds and of the unusual motions among the draperies.

One night, near the end of September, she called my attention with more than usual emphasis to this subject. She had just awakened from an unquiet slumber, and I had been watching, with feelings half of anxiety, half of vague terror, the workings of her thin face. She partly arose and spoke in an earnest low whisper of sounds which she *then* heard, but which I could not hear; of motions which she *then* saw, but which I could not perceive. The wind was moving behind the draperies, and I wished to show her (though I confess I was not entirely sure of it myself) that the breathings she heard, the movement of the figures on the wall, were purely natural effects of the wind. Her deadly pallor proved to me that my efforts to reassure her would be useless. She appeared to be fainting, and there were no servants within call. I remembered a decanter of light wine, which had been ordered by her physician, and hastened across the chamber to get it. But, as I stepped beneath the light of the censer, my attention was attracted by two circumstances of a startling nature. I felt as though some actual though invisible object had passed lightly by me; and I saw that there lay upon the golden carpet in the light thrown by the censer a shadow—a faint shadow like that of an angel. Wild with the excitement of opium, I heeded these things but little and did not speak of them to Rowena.

Having found the wine, I recrossed the chamber and

poured out a gobletful, which I held to the lips of the fainting lady. She had now partially recovered, however, and held the cup herself. I sank upon a couch nearby, with my eyes fastened upon her. It was then that I became plainly aware of a gentle footfall upon the carpet and near the couch; and a second thereafter, as Rowena was in the act of raising the wine to her lips, I saw fall within the goblet, as if from some invisible source, three or four drops of a brilliant and ruby-colored fluid. But Rowena, unseeing, swallowed the wine unhesitatingly. I did not speak to her of a circumstance which must after all have been no more than the suggestion of a vivid imagination made even stronger by the terror of the lady, by the opium, and by the hour.

Yet I could not fail to realize that, immediately after the fall of the ruby-red drops, a rapid change for the worse took place in my wife. On the third night following, the hands of her servants prepared her for the tomb; and on the fourth I sat alone with her shrouded body in that fantastic chamber which had received her as my bride. Wild visions, opium-produced, flitted before my eyes. I gazed upon the figures in the drapery and upon the many-colored fires in the censer overhead. Then I recalled to mind a former night when I had seen, on a spot beneath the glare of the censer, the faint traces of a shadow. It was there no longer, and, breathing more freely, I turned my eyes to the figure upon the bed. There rushed upon me a thousand memories of Ligeia—and then came upon my heart the grief with which I had gazed at *her* shrouded form. The night passed; and still with a heart full of bitter thoughts of the one, only, and supremely beloved, I remained gazing upon the body of Rowena.

It might have been midnight, perhaps earlier or later, for I had taken no note of time, when a sob, low, gentle, but very distinct, startled me from my thoughts. I *felt* that it came from the bed of ebony—the bed of death. I listened in an agony of terror, but there was no repetition of the sound. I strained my eyes to detect any motion in the corpse, but there was none. Yet I could not have been deceived. I *had* heard the noise, however faint, and my soul was awakened within me. I riveted my attention upon the body. Many minutes passed by before anything occurred which could throw light on the mystery. At length it became evident that a very feeble and barely noticeable tinge of color had appeared upon Rowena's cheeks and eyelids. With awe and horror I felt my heart cease to beat and my limbs grow rigid. A sense of duty restored my self-possession. I could no longer doubt that we had been too hasty in our preparations—that Rowena still lived. It was necessary that I do something at once; yet the tower was far from the servants' quarters. I had no means of getting aid without leaving the room for many minutes—and this I could not venture to do. I therefore struggled alone in my efforts to restore her. In a short time it was certain that a relapse had taken place; the color disappeared, leaving her paler than marble; her face resumed the pinched and ghastly expression of death. I fell back upon the couch from which I had been so startlingly aroused and again gave myself up to waking visions of Ligeia.

An hour thus passed when (could it be possible?) I was a second time aware of some vague sound coming from the region of the bed. I listened—in extremity of horror. The sound came again—it was a sigh. Rushing to the corpse, I distinctly saw a trembling of the lips. A minute afterwards they opened, showing a bright line of pearly teeth. Amazement now struggled with the awe which I had felt before. My eyes grew dim; my reason wandered; and it was only by a violent effort that I succeeded in nerving myself to the task which duty thus once more had pointed out. There was now a partial glow upon her forehead and upon her cheeks and throat; a definite warmth came upon her whole figure; there was even a slight palpitation of the heart. The lady *lived;* and with renewed zeal I took means to restore her. I rubbed and bathed her temples and her hands and used every means which my experience and medical knowledge could suggest. But in vain. Suddenly the color fled, her pulse ceased, her lips resumed the expression of the dead, and in an instant afterward her whole body took on the icy chillness of those who have been long in the tomb.

And again I was lost in visions of Ligeia, and again (what wonder I shudder as I write!) *again* there reached my ears a low sob from the region of the ebony bed. But why should I give all the details of that night of unspeakable horror? Why should I tell how, time after time, until gray dawn, this hideous drama was repeated; how each relapse went into a colder death; how each agony seemed to be a struggle with some invisible foe; how each struggle was followed by some wild change in the appearance of the corpse. Let me hurry to a conclusion.

The greater part of the fearful night had worn away, and she who had been dead once again stirred, now more vigorously than before, although from an appearance of death more total than any before. I had long ceased to move and remained sitting rigidly upon the couch. The corpse, I repeat, stirred now more vigorously than before. Signs of life returned to the face, the limbs relaxed, and, except that the eyelids were pressed heavily together, and the draperies of the grave were still there, I might have dreamed that Rowena had indeed shaken off completely the chains of death. This I could doubt no longer when, arising from the bed, with feeble steps, with closed eyes, and with the manner of one in a dream, she advanced into the middle of the chamber.

I did not tremble. I did not stir, for a crowd of unspeakable ideas about the manner, the figure, the whole appearance of the lady rushing through my brain had paralyzed me into stone. There was a mad tumult in my thoughts. Could it indeed be the living Rowena *at all*—the fair-haired, the blue-eyed Lady Rowena Trevanian of Tremaine? Why, why should I doubt it? Was that not her mouth? And the flushed cheeks—these might indeed be the fair ones of the living Lady of Tremaine. And the chin, with its dimples, might it not be hers? But *had she then grown taller* since her fatal illness? What madness seized me at that thought? With one bound I reached her. Shrinking from me, she let fall from her head the draperies of the grave which had covered it, and there streamed forth huge masses of hair; *it was blacker than midnight*. And now slowly the eyes of the figure which stood before me opened. "Here then, at last," I shrieked aloud, "I can never be mistaken. These are the full and black and wild eyes of my lost love—of the Lady—of the Lady Ligeia."

What were her last words? "Man does not let himself die unless his will is too weak to conquer death." Then I knew that all night long I had been watching the struggles of that strong will to triumph over death and the Lady Rowena. Ligeia had come back to me.

# THE FALL OF THE HOUSE OF USHER

DURING the whole of a dull, dark day, in the autumn of the year, when the clouds hung low in the heavens, I had been passing alone, on horseback, through a dreary tract of country. At length, as evening approached, I found myself within view of the melancholy House of Usher. I know not why it was, but with my first glimpse of the building a sense of unbearable gloom overcame me. I looked upon the house, with its bleak walls, its vacant, eye-like windows, and its weed-grown lawns, with a sinking of heart and a dreariness of mind unrelieved by any ray of hope. What was it—I stopped to think—what was it that so horrified me at the sight of the House of Usher? It was a mystery I could not solve. I reined my horse at the edge of a black and stagnant pond and gazed down with a shudder at the image of the house reflected on its surface.

Nevertheless, in this gloomy mansion I now planned to stay for several weeks. Its owner, Roderick Usher, had been one of my boyhood companions, though many years had passed since our last meeting. A letter from him, however, had lately reached me in a distant part of the country. The writer of it spoke of severe bodily illness, and of a desire to see me, his only personal friend. I could do nothing else but obey his unusual summons and started out at once.

Although we had been intimate as boys, I really knew little about my friend. He had always been extremely reserved. I knew, however, that his very ancient family had been long noted for its works of art; its deeds of quiet but remarkably generous charity; its passionate love of music. I had learned, too, the striking fact that no member of the family had lived to be very old. For generations the inheritance had passed directly from father to son. There seemed to be no other living relations. Perhaps that was why the "House of Usher" meant, in the minds of those who referred to it, both the estate itself and the people who had inherited it.

All this I thought of as I stood looking down into the water. When I at length lifted my eyes up to the house itself, a strange feeling came over me. It seemed to me there was an unearthly atmosphere over everything, a threat that came from the decayed trees, the gray walls, and the stagnant pond.

Shaking off these fancies, I scanned the building more closely. It was extremely old, though in no way dilapidated. Moss covered its walls; but none of them had as yet started to crumble. A careful observer could see a slight crack which, starting at the roof of the building in front, extended downward in a zigzag direction to the waters of the pond. Beyond this, there were no indications of decay.

Observing these things, I rode over a short causeway to the house. A servant took my horse, and I entered the hall. A valet then led me in silence through many dark and winding passages to the studio of his master. Much that I saw on the way added to the vague fears of which I have already spoken. On the surface the furnishings were the ordinary objects to which I had become accustomed from my earliest youth—carved ceilings, tapestry-covered walls, antique weapons, and suits of armor. Yet they stirred within me unfamiliar imaginings. On one of the staircases I met the physician of the family. His face, I thought, wore a look of slyness and bewilderment. He greeted me with apparent fear and then passed on. The valet threw open a door and ushered me into the presence of his master.

The room in which I found myself was very large and lofty. The windows were long, narrow, and pointed, and at a tremendous distance from the floor. Feeble gleams of light came through the stained glass and showed up with sufficient distinctness the objects nearest to me. Remote corners of the room and angles in the ceiling were dim. Dark draperies hung upon the walls.

The furniture was comfortless, antique, and tattered. Many books and musical instruments were scattered about, but failed to give the room a home-like quality. I felt that I was breathing an atmosphere of sorrow. An air of stern, deep, and total gloom hung over all.

Upon my entrance, Usher arose from a sofa on which he had been lying at full length and greeted me with what seemed to me at first a forced cordiality. A glance at his face, however, convinced me of his perfect sincerity. We sat down; and for some moments, while he did not speak, I gazed at him with a feeling half of pity, half of awe. Surely a man had never before so terribly changed in so brief a period as had Roderick Usher. It was with difficulty that I could identify the pale being before me as the companion of my early boyhood. Yet the character of his face had been at all times remarkable. A pale complexion; eyes large and bright beyond comparison; lips thin and pale but beautifully curved; a nose of a delicate Hebrew type but with broad nostrils; a finely-moulded chin, showing by its weakness a lack of moral energy; hair of great softness and fineness—these features, with an unusually high forehead, made up a countenance not easily to be forgotten. And all these had been exaggerated by the years during which I had not seen him. The ghastly pallor of his skin and the strange gleam in his eyes startled and awed me. His silken hair had been allowed to grow unnoticed and floated rather than fell about his face.

In the manner of my friend, too, I was struck with

something strange; and I soon found this to arise from his attempt to conceal from me extreme nervous agitation. For something of this sort I had been prepared both by his letter and by my recollection of his boyish traits and temperament. His attitude was alternately lively and sullen. His voice varied from trembling indecision to abrupt and hollow-sounding firmness.

It was thus that he spoke of the object of my visit, of his earnest desire to see me, and of the comfort he expected me to be to him. He discussed at some length what he thought was the nature of his illness. It was, he said, an inherited weakness for which he despaired of finding a remedy—a nervous affliction which would soon pass off. It showed itself in a host of unnatural feelings. Some of these, as he described them, bewildered me. He suffered from extreme sensitiveness; only the simplest food was endurable; he could wear only garments of a certain texture; the odors of all flowers were oppressive; his eyes were tortured by even a faint light; and there were few sounds, except the music of stringed instruments, which did not inspire him with horror.

He was a slave to nameless terrors. "I shall die," said he, "in this regrettable folly. Thus and not otherwise shall I be lost. I dread the events of the future, not in themselves, but in their results. I shudder at the thought of any, even the most trifling, happening which might upset me. I have no dread of actual danger—only of my fear of it. In this condition I feel that the time will sooner or later arrive when I must give up life and reason together in some struggle with the grim ghost, Fear."

I learned at intervals, through occasional hints, another singular characteristic of his mental condition. He had certain superstitious feelings in regard to the dwelling in which he lived and from which in many years he had not ventured forth. He felt a peculiar influence that it was exerting on him—as though the gray walls and towers and the dim pond in which they were reflected had at length affected his whole existence.

He admitted, however, though with hesitation, that much of the peculiar gloom which thus afflicted him had a more natural cause—the severe and long-continued illness, possibly even the approaching death of a dearly loved sister, his sole companion for many years, his last relative on earth. "Her death," he said, with a bitterness I can never forget, "would leave me—me the hopeless and the frail—the last of the ancient race of the Ushers."

While he spoke, the Lady Madeline (for so was she called) passed slowly through a distant part of the room and, without having noticed my presence, disappeared. I looked at her with utter astonishment, not unmixed with dread, and yet I found it impossible to account for such feelings. When she had gone, I looked anxiously at the brother; but he had buried his face in his hands, and I could see only that passionate tears trickled through his pale fingers.

The disease of the Lady Madeline had long baffled

her physicians. A settled lifelessness, a gradual wasting away, and frequent spells of a cataleptic[1] nature were the usual diagnoses. Hitherto she had fought against her sickness and had not taken to her bed; but upon the night of my arrival at the house, she gave in to the power of her destroyer. I learned that the glimpse I had had of her would probably be my last one—that the lady, at least while she was still living, would be seen by me no more.

For several days following, her name was not mentioned by either Usher or me; and during this period I was busy with my efforts to cheer my friend. We painted and read together; or I listened as if in a dream to the wild melodies of his guitar. And thus, as I came closer to him, the more bitterly did I see the uselessness of all attempts at cheering a mind from which darkness poured on all things in his universe.

I shall always remember the many solemn hours I spent alone with the master of the House of Usher. Yet I cannot recall the exact nature of the studies or the occupations with which we spent our time. Among other things I remember his playing the wild air of the last waltz of Von Weber. I remember the weirdness of the paintings his imagination led him to make. One in particular, I remember, showed the interior of an immensely long and rectangular vault or tunnel, with low walls, smooth, white, and plain. It conveyed the idea that it lay at a great depth below the surface of the

[1] Catalepsy—A sort of fit in which the victim loses consciousness and becomes rigid.

earth. There was no outlet in any portion of its vast extent and no artificial source of light to be seen; yet a flood of intense rays bathed the whole in a ghastly splendor.

I have said before that all music was unbearable to the sufferer but that of stringed instruments. The fantastic character of his performance on the guitar was unbelievable. Sometimes he accompanied his playing with rhymed verses he had composed. The words of one of these I have easily remembered. In it I saw for the first time a realization on his part that his reason was gradually leaving him! The verses, which were entitled "The Haunted Palace," ran like this:

*I*

[1]*In the greenest of our valleys*
*By good angels tenanted,*
*Once a fair and stately palace—*
*Radiant palace—reared its head.*
*In the monarch Thought's dominion,*
*It stood there;*
*Never seraph spread a pinion*
*Over fabric half so fair.*

*II*

*Banners yellow, glorious, golden,*
*On its roof did float and flow,*

[1] Of this poem Poe says, "I meant to describe a mind haunted by phantoms—a disordered brain."

*(This—all this—was in the olden*
*Time long ago)*
*And every gentle air that dallied,*
*In that sweet day,*
*Along the ramparts plumed and pallid*
*A winged odor went away.*

III

*Wanderers in that happy valley*
*Through two luminous windows saw*
*Spirits moving musically*
*To a lute's well-tuned law,*
*Round about a throne where, sitting,*
*[1]Porphyrogene,*
*In state his glory well befitting,*
*The ruler of the realm was seen.*

IV

*And all with pearl and ruby glowing*
*Was the fair palace door,*
*Through which came flowing, flowing, flowing,*
*And sparkling evermore,*
*A troop of Echoes whose sweet duty*
*Was but to sing,*
*In voices of surpassing beauty,*
*The wit and wisdom of their king.*

[1] A royal prince.

V

*But evil things in robes of sorrow*
*Assailed the monarch's high estate;*
*(Ah, let us mourn, for never morrow*
*Shall dawn upon him, desolate!)*
*And round about his home the glory*
*That blushed and bloomed*
*Is but a dim-remembered story*
*Of the old time entombed.*

VI

*And travellers now within that valley*
*Through the red-litten windows see*
*Vast forms that move fantastically*
*To a discordant melody;*
*While, like a ghastly rapid river,*
*Through the pale door*
*A hideous throng rush out forever,*
*And laugh—but smile no more.*

While we were thinking about this ballad, I well remember an idea of Usher's, which I mention not so much on account of its novelty as on account of the persistence with which he held to it. His opinion, in its general form, was that all the lifeless objects around him had thought and feeling of their own. This belief seemed to be somehow connected with the gray stones of the home of his forefathers. The moss-covered castle itself, the decayed trees which stood around it, the many years it had lasted, even its reflection in the still waters of the lake seemed to give out a peculiar atmosphere of their own. The result was shown, he said, in the terrible influence which had formed the fate of his family and which had made him into what he was.

Our books were in strict keeping with his state of mind. For many years they had been almost his sole companions—plays, poetry, philosophy, history. Many were fantastic in their ideas; all contributed to the strangeness of his mind. I could not help thinking of the wildness of some of these books and their probable influence on the invalid, when one evening he informed me abruptly that the Lady Madeline had died. He stated his intention of preserving her corpse for a fortnight, before its final burial, in one of the numerous vaults within the main walls of the building. The reason given for this unusual proceeding was one which I could not disagree with. He had been led to his resolution (so he told me) by the unusual nature of his sister's disease, by certain persistent questions on the part of her doctor, and by the distant and exposed situation of the family burial-ground. When I recalled the sinister face of the person whom had I met on the staircase the day of my arrival at the house, I had no desire to oppose what I considered a harmless and by no means unnatural precaution.

At the request of Usher, I aided him in the preparations for the temporary burial. The body having been put in its coffin, we two alone carried it to its rest. The vault in which we placed it, which had been long unopened, was small, damp, and entirely without light. It lay far below that portion of the building in which I had my sleeping quarters. It had been used in early days as the worst sort of prison, and in later days as a place to store powder or some other explosive. A portion of its floor and the whole inside of a long archway through which we reached it were sheathed with copper. The door, of massive iron, had been similarly protected. Its immense weight caused it to give a sharp, grating sound as it moved on its hinges.

Having placed our mournful burden within this region of horror, we partially opened the lid of the coffin and gazed at the face of the Lady Madeline. A striking likeness between the brother and sister first caught my attention. Usher, somehow guessing my thoughts, let me know that they were twins and that a deep sympathy had always existed between them. Our glances rested for only a short time upon the dead; we were too much awed by the sight. The disease had struck the lady while she was still young. It had left, as is usual with catalepsy, a faint blush upon her face and a lingering smile upon her lips. We replaced and screwed down the lid of the coffin, closed the iron door, and made our way into the scarcely less gloomy rooms of the upper portion of the house.

And now, after some days of bitter grief had passed by, a change came over my friend. His ordinary manner was gone. His ordinary occupations were neglected or forgotten. He wandered from room to room with hurried and purposeless steps. His pale face had grown if possible even paler. But the glow in his eyes had utterly gone out. The once occasional huskiness of his tone was heard no more, being replaced by a tremulous quaver as if of extreme terror. There were times, indeed, when I thought his agitated mind was laboring with some burdensome secret which he lacked the necessary courage to confess. At times again I could only think him mad, for I saw him gazing into vacancy for long hours in an attitude of attention, as if listening to some imaginary sound. It was no wonder that he terrified me. I felt creeping upon me by slow yet certain degrees the wild influences of his fantastic superstitions.

Upon retiring to bed late in the night of the seventh or eighth day after placing the Lady Madeline in the dungeon, I experienced the full power of such feelings. Sleep would not come to me hour after hour. I struggled to reason away the nervousness which held power over me. I tried to believe that much, if not all, of what I felt was due to the influence of the gloomy furniture of the room and of the dark and tattered draperies which, blown by a rising tempest, swayed to and fro upon the walls and rustled uneasily about the decorations of the bed. But my efforts were in vain. I gradually began to tremble and to have a feeling of utterly causeless alarm. Shaking this off with difficulty, I sat up and peered earnestly into the darkness of my room. I listened—I know not why, except that something prompted me—to certain low and indefinite sounds which came, through the pauses of the storm, at long intervals. Overpowered by a feeling of horror, I threw on my clothes with haste and tried to calm myself by walking rapidly to and fro in my room.

I had taken but a few turns in this manner when a light step arrested my attention. I recognized it as that of Usher. An instant later he rapped at my door and entered, bearing a lamp. His face was, as usual, pale as that of a corpse, but now there was a sort of wild madness in his eyes. His manner appalled me. But anything was better than the solitude which I had endured so long, and I even welcomed his presence with relief.

"You have not seen it?" he said abruptly, after having stared about him for several moments in silence. "You have not then seen it? But wait. You shall." Thus speaking, having carefully shaded his lamp, he hurried to one of the windows and threw it open to the storm.

The fury of the entering gust nearly lifted us from our feet. It was a wild yet sternly beautiful night. A wind was blowing with full force around the castle, altering its direction frequently and violently. The thick clouds hung so low as to press upon the towers of the house. We had no glimpse of moon or stars, nor were there any flashes of lightning. But the under surfaces of the huge clouds, as well as objects on the ground, were glowing in the unnatural light of faintly luminous mists which hung about the mansion.

"You must not—you shall not behold this!" said I, shudderingly, to Usher, as I led him from the window. "These sights which bewilder you are merely electrical phenomena, not uncommon. It may be that they come from the rank dampness of the pond. Let us close this window; the air is chilling and dangerous to you. Here is one of your favorite romances. I will read and you shall listen. And so we will pass this terrible night together."

The old volume I had taken up was one called the *Mad Trist*, by Sir Launcelot Canning. It was the only book at hand, and I had a vague hope that the excitement which now filled him might find relief in what I would now read. If I could have judged by the overstrained interest with which he listened, or apparently listened, to the words of the tale, I might well have congratulated myself on the success of my plan.

I arrived at the part in the story where Ethelred, the hero, having tried in vain to enter the home of a hermit peaceably, had to force his way in. The words of the narrative run as follows:

"And Ethelred, always brave, and now strong from the wine he had drunk, refused to talk longer with the hermit, who, through malice, was refusing him entrance. Feeling the rain on his shoulders and fearing the rising storm, he lifted his mace and broke through the boards of the door. The noise of the dry and hollow-sounding wood echoed throughout the forest."

At the end of this sentence I started and for a moment paused. It seemed to me that from some very remote region of the mansion there came indistinctly to my ears what might have been the very echo of the cracking and ripping sound which Sir Launcelot had described. It was, beyond doubt, the coincidence which had attracted my attention; for, amid the rattling of the windows and the noises of the still increasing storm, the sound itself held nothing, surely, which should have interested or disturbed me. I continued with the story.

"But the champion Ethelred, entering the door, was enraged to see no sign of the hermit, but instead a scaly dragon sitting in guard before a palace of gold. Ethelred lifted his mace and struck the head of the dragon, who fell before him with a harsh shriek, so piercing that Ethelred covered his ears with his hands to shut out the dreadful noise, the like of which he had never heard before."

Here again I paused abruptly, now with a feeling of wild amazement. There could be no doubt whatever that in this case I did actually hear, although from what direction it came I could not say, a distant but harsh, long, and most unusual screaming or grating sound, exactly like what I imagined to be the dragon's shriek described by the writer.

Oppressed as I was by this second strange coincidence, and filled with wonder and terror, I still kept enough presence of mind to avoid exaggerating the already extreme nervousness of my companion. I was not sure that he had noticed the sounds, although a strange alteration in his manner had taken place in the last few minutes. From a position in front of me, he had gradually brought his chair around so that he could face the door of the room; thus I could only partially see his face. I observed that his lips trembled as though he were murmuring. His head had dropped upon his breast; yet I knew from his wide and rigidly opened eyes that he was not asleep. He rocked from side to side with a gentle yet constant sway. I proceeded with the narrative of Sir Launcelot.

"Now the champion, having escaped the terrible fury of the dragon, pushed its carcass out of his way and advanced to the wall where the shield was. As he approached, it fell down at his feet with a great and terrible ringing sound."

No sooner had these words passed my lips than I became aware of a hollow, metallic, yet apparently muffled sound. Completely unnerved, I leaped to my feet; but the rocking movement of Usher was undisturbed. I rushed to the chair in which he sat. His eyes stared fixedly before him, and his whole face kept its stony calm. But, as I placed my hand upon his shoulder, a strong shudder came over him; a sickly smile quivered about his lips; and I saw that he spoke in a low murmur as if unconscious of my presence. Bending closer, I at length heard his hideous words.

"Not hear? Yes, I hear it and *have* heard it. Long–long–long–many minutes, many hours, many days have I heard it– Yet I dared not–miserable wretch that I am–I *dared* not speak! *We have put her living in the tomb!* Did I not say my senses were keen? I heard her first feeble movements in the hollow coffin. I heard them many, many days ago. *Yet I dared not speak.* And, now tonight–Ethelred, the breaking of the hermit's door, the death-cry of the dragon, the clang of the shield

—say, rather, the rending of her coffin, the grating of the iron hinges of her prison, and her struggle within the copper archway of the vault! Where shall I fly? Will she not be here at once? Have I not heard her footstep on the stair? Do I not recognize the heavy and horrible beating of her heart?—Madman!"—he sprang furiously to his feet and shrieked out the syllables—"Madman, *I tell you that she now stands outside the door!"*

As if his utterance had the force of a spell, the huge antique panels of the door at which Usher pointed slowly opened. Outside stood the tall figure of the Lady Madeline, wrapped in her shroud. There was blood upon her white robes and the evidence of bitter struggle about her person. For a moment she remained trembling and reeling to and fro upon the threshold. Then, with a low moaning cry, she fell heavily inward upon her brother, and in her final and now violent death-agonies, bore him to the floor a corpse—killed by the terrors which had for so long tormented him, and by remorse over the terror which had made him incapable of rescuing her from the tomb.

From that room and from that mansion I fled in horror. The storm was still raging as I crossed the old causeway. Suddenly there shot along the path a wild light, and I turned to see where it could have come from, for the vast house and its shadows were alone behind me. The radiance was that of the full moon, blood-red at its setting. Its light shone vividly through that once slight crack of which I have before spoken as extending from the roof of the building in a zigzag direction to the base.

While I gazed, the crack widened rapidly. There came a fierce gust of wind. The full moon burst at once upon my sight. My brain reeled as I saw the mighty walls of the castle separating. There was a long shouting sound like the voice of a thousand waters. And the deep and dark pond at my feet closed sullenly and silently over the ruins of the House of Usher.

# *Old Legends Are Recalled*

# MS. FOUND IN A BOTTLE

I HAVE very little to say about my country and my family. Misfortune and long absence have separated me from both. Because I inherited wealth, I was able to get a good education, which I have improved upon by continued interest in learning. Science has always attracted me greatly, and I enjoy explaining by its rules unusual things which occur. I am not easily influenced by superstition. The remarkable tale I have to tell should not, then, be considered the ravings of a crude imagination, but rather a real experience of a person whose mind is free from idle fancies.

After many years spent in foreign travel, I sailed in the year 18— from the port of Batavia, on the rich island of Java, on a voyage to the islands of the South Polar

Sea. I went as a passenger seeking adventure because of a nervous restlessness which haunted me all the time.

Our vessel was a beautiful one of about four hundred tons, built in Bombay. Her cargo was cotton-wool, oil, cocoanuts, and a few cases of opium. It was stowed away with so little system that the ship was consequently badly balanced.

We started out on a mere breath of wind and for many days idled along the coast of Java. Nothing broke the monotony but an occasional meeting with small cargo boats back from the same lands for which we were heading.

One evening when I was leaning over the rail and gazing out to sea, I noticed a very peculiar cloud in the northwest. It was the first one we had seen since we left Batavia and was of a remarkable color. I watched it attentively until sunset, when it spread all at once both eastward and westward, forming a narrow strip of mist and looking like a long line of low beach. Soon after that I noticed that the moon had a dark red appearance. The sea looked peculiar, too; the water seemed more transparent than usual. Although I could distinctly see the bottom, I discovered, when I had taken soundings, that the water was fifteen fathoms deep.

The air now became unbearably hot. As night came on, every breath of wind died away. The sea was so completely calm that the flame of a candle burned without any motion at all, and a long hair held between finger and thumb did not even vibrate. As the captain said he could see no sign of danger, and as we were drifting in to shore, he ordered the sails to be furled and the anchor to be dropped. No watch was set, and the crew, composed chiefly of Malays, stretched themselves out on deck. I went below—not feeling entirely safe. Every appearance made me fear a hurricane. I told the captain how I felt, but he paid no attention to what I said and left me without even replying. My uneasiness, however, prevented me from sleeping, and about midnight I went up on deck. As I placed my foot upon the upper step of the ladder, I was startled by a loud humming noise. Before I could find out what it meant, I found the ship quivering all over. In an instant a wilderness of foam, rushing fore and aft, swept the entire decks from stem to stern.

The extreme fury of the blast was in great measure the salvation of the ship. Although completely waterlogged, yet as her masts were swept away, she rose heavily from the sea. Staggering awhile under the pressure of the tempest, she finally righted.

It is impossible to say by what miracle I escaped destruction. Stunned by the shock of the water, I regained my feet with great difficulty, and, looking dizzily around, at first thought that we were among breakers, so terrific was the mountainous and foaming ocean all around us.

After a while I heard the voice of an old Swede, who had shipped with us just as we were leaving port. I called out to him with all my strength, and he came reeling toward me. We discovered that we were the sole survivors of the accident. Everyone else on deck had been swept overboard; the captain and the mates must have died while they slept, for their cabins were filled with water.

Without aid we could do little to make the ship safe. At first we did nothing, for we expected to go down any minute. We had, of course, broken anchor when the hurricane hit us, and we were driven along with frightful speed, the waves breaking over us constantly. We discovered to our extreme joy, however, that the pumps were undamaged and that our ballast had shifted very little. The main fury of the blast had already blown over, and we no longer dreaded the violence of the wind, though it blew for five entire days and nights, sending us before it with considerable speed.

Our course for the first four days was southeast and by south, and we must have run down the coast of the Dutch East Indies. On the fifth day the cold became extreme, although the wind had shifted a little more to the northward. The sun rose with a sickly yellow glow and climbed a few degrees above the horizon, giving no clear light. There were no clouds; yet the wind increased and blew with unsteady fury. About noon, as clearly as we could guess, our attention was again attracted by the appearance of the sun. It gave out no actual light, but a dull and sullen glow without reflection. Just before it sank, its fires went out suddenly, as if put out by some strange power.

We waited in vain for the coming of the sixth day. That day to me has not yet arrived. To the Swede it never did arrive. For we were wrapped in such complete darkness that we could not see an object twenty paces from us. We were in the midst of eternal night. We noticed, too, that although the wind continued to rage fiercely, there was no longer surf or foam in the ocean. All around us were horror and gloom and a black waste of waters. The old Swede was filled with superstitious terror, and I was silent with wonder. We neglected all care of the ship as worse than useless; tying ourselves to what was left of a mast, we looked out into the world of ocean. We had no way of figuring either the time or our position. We were aware, however, that we had gone farther south than any sailors ever had before, and we were amazed that we had not met with any icebergs. Meanwhile, every moment threatened to sink us. My companion reminded me of the excellence of our ship and of the lightness of our cargo; but I felt utterly hopeless and prepared myself for the death which I thought certain. Every hour the waves became higher, and we became more dizzy with the speed of our ascents and descents.

We were at the bottom of one of these vast swells when a quick scream from my companion was heard. "Look! look!" he cried, shrieking in my ears. "Almighty God, look!" As he spoke I saw a dull glare of red light which streamed down the sides of the vast mountain of water at the bottom of which we lay and threw a brief glow on our decks. At a terrific height directly above us and upon the very edge of the steep descent was a gigantic ship. Although she was upon the summit of a wave more than a hundred times her own height, she looked larger than any other ship in existence. Her huge hull was a dingy black. A single row of brass cannon stuck out from her open port holes. Numerous battle lanterns were hung in her rigging. What chiefly amazed and horrified us was that she was in full sail in spite of that gigantic sea and that raging hurricane. When we first discovered her, her bows alone were to be seen as she rose from the gulf beyond her. For a moment she paused on the peak of the wave, then trembled and tottered and—came down!

A great calmness came to me suddenly. Fearlessly I awaited ruin. Our own ship had at length ceased to struggle and was sinking, with her head to the sea. When she was struck by the huge descending mass of the other ship, I was hurled with violence upon the rigging of the stranger.

As I fell, the ship turned about. In the confusion I must have escaped the notice of the crew. With little difficulty I made my way unnoticed to the main hatchway, which was partly open, and hid myself in the hold. Why I did so I can hardly tell, though it was partly because I felt a queer sense of awe at first sight of the sailors on the other ship. I was unwilling to trust myself to people who filled me with such doubt and fear. So I made myself a hiding-place between the huge timbers of the ship by removing some boards that would not be noticed.

I had scarcely finished my work when the sound of a footstep forced me to use my retreat. A man passed by, walking feebly and unsteadily. I could not see his face, but he seemed old and weak. He muttered to himself in a language I could not understand and groped in a corner among a pile of queer-looking instruments and decayed charts. He at length went on deck, and I did not see him any more.

It is a long time since I first arrived on this terrible ship, and I feel that something is about to happen. Strange men! Wrapped in thought, they pass me by unnoticed. I do not need to hide myself, for the people *will* not see me. Just now I passed directly in front of the mate; not long ago I went into the captain's own private cabin and carried away the materials with which I am writing. I shall continue this journal from time to time. Perhaps I shall never find a chance to give it to the world, but I will try. At the last moment I will put the manuscript in a bottle and cast it into the sea.

Lately I have observed the structure of the vessel. Although armed, she is not, I think, a ship of war. It is far easier to tell what she is not than what she is. When I look at her strange shape, her huge size, and her vast sails, I have a sense of familiar things mixed with a memory of old foreign chronicles and ages long gone.

I have been looking at the timbers of the ship. I do not recognize the material of which she is built. The wood does not seem appropriate for a ship. It is too porous—almost like Spanish oak, which has been swelled by some unnatural means.

That makes me remember something an old Dutch

navigator used to say: "Somewhere there is a sea where ships grow larger as they sail upon it."

About an hour ago I joined a group of the crew. They paid no attention to me and seemed utterly unconscious of my presence. Like the one I had first seen, they were all very, very old. Their knees trembled; their shoulders were bent double; their voices were low and trembling; their gray hairs streamed in the wind. On the deck lay antique mathematical instruments.

The ship continues her course due south. She carries full sail and rolls every minute through the most terrible sea man could imagine. I have just left the deck, where I cannot keep my footing, though the crew seems to find it no difficulty. It seems to me a miracle that we are not swallowed up by the sea at once and forever. We are surely doomed to continue always on the edge of destruction without taking the fatal plunge. We glide away with the ease of a sea-gull from waves a thousand times higher than any I have ever seen before. The waters rear their heads above us like demons of the deep, but like demons that will always threaten and never destroy. I seek for some natural cause for these frequent escapes. The ship may be under the influence of some strong current or some violent undertow.

I have seen the Captain face to face and in his own cabin, but, as I expected, he paid no attention to me. For some reason that I cannot explain he filled me with a feeling of reverence and awe. In height he is about five feet eight inches. He is well built, neither robust nor frail. It is the expression on his face that is most impressive. Utter and extreme old age is reflected there. His gray hairs are records of the past; his gray eyes look into the future. The cabin floor was strewn with strange old folios and mouldy instruments of science and ancient charts. His head was bowed upon his hands, and he gazed upon a paper which was signed by a monarch. He murmured to himself in a foreign tongue; and although he was close at my elbow, his voice seemed to reach my ears from the distance of a mile.

The crew glide by me like ghosts of buried centuries. I feel as I have never felt before, though all my life I have been a student of ancient days and ancient men. About the ship is the blackness of eternal night and a wilderness of foamless water; but on either side of us may be seen indistinctly and at intervals huge ramparts of ice, towering away into the desolate sky and looking like the walls of the universe.

As I imagined, the ship is in a current, if such a title can be given to a tide, which, howling and shrieking by the white ice, thunders southward with the violence of a waterfall.

It is impossible to imagine the horror of my feelings. Yet my curiosity to explore the mysteries of these awful regions is stronger than my despair and will reconcile me to the most hideous death. We are hurrying onward to some exciting secret whose knowledge is destruction. Perhaps this current leads us to the South Pole itself.

The crew pace the deck with trembling steps, but there is on their faces an expression more of hope than of despair.

In the meantime the wind is still with us, and, as we carry so much canvas, the ship is at times lifted bodily out of the sea. But horror of horrors! The ice opens suddenly to the right and to the left, and we are whirling dizzily in immense circles, round and round the borders of a gigantic amphitheatre, the top of whose walls is lost in the darkness and the distance. I will have little time to think about my fate. The circles grow rapidly smaller. We are plunging madly into the whirlpool. Amid a roaring and a thundering of ocean and tempest, the ship is trembling and—going down!

# THE MASQUE OF THE RED DEATH

THE RED DEATH had long laid waste the country. No plague had ever been so fatal or so hideous. Blood was the sign of its progress—the redness and the horror of blood. Its victims felt sharp pains, sudden dizziness, profuse bleeding, and then death. The scarlet stains upon the body and especially upon the face of the victim were the signs which shut him out from the aid and from the sympathy of his fellow-men. And the whole start, progress, and end of the disease took place within half an hour.

But the Prince Prospero was happy and fearless and wise. When half the people in his realm had died, he summoned a thousand healthy and light-hearted friends from among the knights and ladies of his court, and with these withdrew to one of his isolated castles in the country. This was an enormous and magnificent building in accordance with the Prince's odd yet dignified taste. A strong and lofty wall, with gates of iron, surrounded it. Having entered, the courtiers closed and welded all the bolts. They planned to leave means neither of entrance nor exit for anyone seized by frenzy or despair. The castle was well stocked with food and drink.

With these precautions the courtiers could defy contagion. The outside world could take care of itself. Meanwhile, it was folly to think or to grieve. The Prince had provided all types of pleasure. There were clowns; there were ballet-dancers; there were musicians; there were beautiful women; there was wine. All these and security were within. Outside was the "Red Death."

It was toward the close of the fifth or sixth month of his seclusion, and while the plague raged most furiously abroad, that Prince Prospero entertained his thousand friends at a masked ball of the most unusual magnificence.

It was a lavish scene, that masquerade. But first let me describe the rooms in which it was held. There were seven of them. In many palaces such suites form a long and straight vista, while folding-doors slide back nearly to the walls on either hand, so that a view of the entire scene is afforded. Here the case was very different, as might be expected from the Prince's love of the fantastic. The apartments here were so irregularly located that the revelers could see but little more than one room at a time. There was a sharp turn every twenty or thirty yards, and at each turn a novel effect. To the right and left, in the middle of each wall, a tall and narrow window looked out upon a closed corridor, which ran throughout the suite. These windows were of stained glass, whose color matched that of the decorations of the room which included them. The first or eastern one was, for example, in blue—and vividly blue were its windows. The second room was purple in its ornaments and tapestries, and here the window panes were purple. The third was green throughout. The fourth was furnished and lighted with orange, the fifth was white, the sixth violet.

But the seventh chamber was closely hung with black velvet tapestries that covered the ceiling and the walls, falling in heavy folds upon a carpet of the same material and hue. In this chamber only, the color of the windows failed to correspond with the decorations. The panes here were scarlet—a deep blood color.

In no one of the seven apartments was there any lamp or candelabrum amid the profusion of golden ornaments that adorned the rooms. But in the corridors from which the chambers opened there stood, opposite each window, a heavy tripod bearing a brazier of fire that cast its rays through the tinted glass and so glaringly illuminated the room—and thus were produced a multitude of gaudy and fantastic shapes. But in the black or western room the effect of the fire light that streamed upon the dark hangings through the blood-tinted panes was ghastly in the extreme, and produced so wild a look upon the faces of those that entered that there were few of the company bold enough to set foot within it.

In this apartment there stood against the western wall a gigantic clock of ebony. Its pendulum swung to and fro with a dull, heavy, monotonous clang; and when the hour was due to strike, there came from the brazen lungs of the clock a sound which was clear and loud and deep and musical, but of so peculiar a note and emphasis that each hour the musicians in the orchestra were forced to pause in their playing and listen to the sound. Thus the waltzers ceased their turning about. Silence fell upon the whole company. While the chimes of the clock still rang, it was seen that the giddiest grew pale, and the more aged and dignified passed their hands over their brows as if in confused meditation. But when the echoes had fully ceased, light laughter at once prevailed. The musicians looked at each other and smiled as if at their own nervousness and folly, and made vows to each other that the next chiming of the clock should have no effect upon them. Then, after the lapse of sixty minutes, when there came still another chiming of the clock, there were the same discord and fear and meditation as before.

In spite of these things, it was a gay and magnificent celebration. The Prince had a fine eye for colors and effects. He had directed in great part the movable decorations of the seven rooms, and it was his guiding taste which was seen in the whole bold masquerade. There were glare and glitter and noise and revelry. There was much that was beautiful, something of the terrible, and not a little so extreme as to be disgusting.

But to the chamber in the west none of the maskers ventured; for the night was passing by, and there flowed a redder light through the blood-colored panes. The blackness of the sable hangings terrified; and to him who stepped upon the sable carpet there came from the clock of ebony a muffled peal.

The other apartments were densely crowded. Here the revel went on, until at length there commenced the sounding of midnight on the clock. Then the music ceased, the dancers paused, and there was uneasy silence as before. But now there were twelve strokes to be sounded by the clock. Thus it happened, perhaps, that there was longer time for meditation among the more thoughtful of the revelers. Thus, too, it happened that many individuals in the crowd had more time to become aware of the presence of a masquerader whom no person had seen before. And, the rumor of this new presence having been whispered about, there arose at length from the whole company a murmur of disapproval and surprise, of terror or horror, and of disgust.

In an assembly such as I have painted, no ordinary appearance could have excited such sensations. In truth the freedom permitted by the masquerade of the night was nearly unlimited. But the figure in question had gone beyond the bounds even of the Prince's standards. The whole company, indeed, seemed now to feel deeply that in the costume and bearing of the stranger there was neither cleverness nor decency. The figure was tall and gaunt, and shrouded from head to foot in grave-clothes. The mask which concealed his face was made so nearly to resemble a stiffened corpse that the closest examination could not have detected the fraud. Yet all this might have been tolerated, if not approved, by the mad revellers. But the mummer had gone so far as to represent the Red Death. His clothing was dabbled with blood and his face sprinkled with the scarlet horror.

When the eyes of Prince Prospero fell upon this spectre, which with slow and solemn movement stalked to and fro among the waltzers, his first sensations were seen to be distaste and terror; his next, rage.

"Who dares," he demanded hoarsely of the courtiers who stood near him, "who dares insult us with this mockery? Seize him and unmask him—so we may know whom to hang from the battlements at sunrise!"

It was the eastern or blue chamber in which stood Prince Prospero as he uttered these words. They rang throughout the seven rooms loudly and clearly, for the Prince was a bold and violent man, and the music had been hushed at the waving of his hand.

It was the blue room where stood the Prince with a group of pale courtiers at his side. At first there was a slight rushing movement in the direction of the intruder, who was near at hand, and who, with deliberate and stately step, approached closer to the speaker. But there were found none who would put a hand forth to seize him. Unhindered, he passed within a yard of the Prince. While the vast assembly shrank back to the walls of the rooms, he made his way, with the same solemn and measured step, through the blue chamber to the purple—through the purple to the green—through the green to the orange—through this again to the white—and thence to the violet, before a decided movement had been made to stop him.

It was then, however, that Prince Prospero, maddened with rage and the shame of his own momentary cowardice, rushed hurriedly through the six chambers, while no one followed him because of a deadly terror that had seized them all. He carried a drawn dagger and had come to within three or four feet of the retreating figure when the latter, having reached the velvet apartment, turned suddenly and confronted his pursuer.

There was a sharp cry, and the dagger dropped gleaming to the sable carpet, upon which, instantly afterward, fell prostrate in death the Prince Prospero. Then, summoning the wild courage of despair, a throng of revellers at once threw themselves into the black apartment and seized the masquerader, whose tall figure stood erect and motionless within the shadow of the ebony clock. In unutterable horror they gasped to find the grave clothes and corpse-like mask inhabited by no human form. The masquerader was a ghost.

And now the presence of the Red Death was acknowledged. He had come like a thief in the night. One by one the revellers dropped in the blood-stained halls and died in despair; and the life of the ebony clock went out with that of the last victim, and the flames of the tripods died out. And Darkness and Decay and the Red Death held endless power over all.

# A DESCENT INTO THE MAELSTRÖM

WE HAD now reached the top of the highest rock. For some minutes the old man with me seemed too tired to speak.

"Not long ago," he said at last, "I could have guided you to this spot with ease. But about three years ago something happened to me that no human being has ever before lived through. Six hours of deadly terror which I endured then have ruined me, body and soul. You consider me a *very* old man—but I am not. It took less than a single day to change my hair from jet black to white, to weaken my body, and to upset my nerves so much that I tremble at the smallest effort and am frightened at a shadow. I can scarcely look over this little cliff without getting dizzy."

The "little cliff" which he mentioned was sheer black rock, which rose fifteen or sixteen hundred feet from the crags below. Nothing would have made me go within half a dozen yards of its edge; yet my companion was sitting so close to it that his body practically hung over. I was terrified that he would fall.

"You must get over these foolish ideas," said my guide. "I have brought you here so that you may get the best possible view of the scene of that experience I mentioned. I am going to tell you the whole story with the spot right under your eyes.

"We are now," he continued, "close to the Norwegian coast. Raise yourself up a little higher. Hold on to the grass if you feel dizzy. Now look out beyond the mist below us into the sea."

I looked dizzily and saw a wide sweep of inky black ocean. No one could imagine a more desolate scene. To the right and left, as far as the eye could see, were lines of black and threatening cliffs beaten at by the surf. Just opposite the crag upon whose top we sat and five or six miles out at sea was a small, black-looking island. Two miles nearer the land was a still smaller one, rough and barren and dotted with clusters of dark rocks.

I saw something unusual about the ocean in the space between the more distant island and the shore. Although a strong gale blew toward land at the time, there was here nothing like a regular swell, but only a short, angry dashing about of water in every direction—

toward the wind as well as away from it. There was little foam except right near the rocks.

"The Norwegians call the island in the distance Vurrgh," continued the old man. "The nearer one is Moskoe. All of them around here are named, though I can see no use for it. Do you hear anything? Do you see any change in the water?"

We had been up there about ten minutes, and in our inland climb had caught no glimpse of the sea until it had burst upon us from the summit. As the old man spoke, I heard a loud and gradually increasing sound, like the moaning of a vast herd of buffaloes on an American prairie. At the same time the choppiness of the ocean beneath us rapidly changed into a current which flowed eastward. Even while I watched, its speed became unbelievable. Each moment it flowed faster. In five minutes the whole sea as far as Vurrgh was lashed into fury; it was worst between Moskoe and the coast. Here the vast waters began to heave and boil and hiss, turning about in deep eddies, all whirling and plunging eastward with a speed which is elsewhere seen only in waterfalls.

In a few minutes more there was another change. The surface of the water became more smooth, and the whirlpools one by one disappeared, while streaks of foam were seen where none had been before. These streaks, spreading out to a great distance and uniting, began to take on a circular motion. Very suddenly they seemed to form a distinct circle, more than a mile in diameter. The edge of this was a broad belt of gleaming spray; but none of this slipped into the mouth of the terrifying funnel, the inside of which, as far as could be seen, was a smooth, shining, and jet-black wall of water, inclined to the horizon at an angle of forty-five degrees, speeding dizzily round and round and sending forth a dreadful sound, half shriek, half roar, far worse than Niagara.

The mountain trembled to its very base, and even the rock on which we sat seemed unsteady. I threw myself upon my face and clung to the bushes around me in terror. "This," I said at last to the old man, "can be nothing else than the great whirlpool of the Maelström."

"So it is sometimes called," said he. "We Norwegians call it the Moskoe-ström, from the island of Moskoe in the middle."

I had read about this before, but the ordinary accounts of it had not prepared me for what I saw. They could not give even the faintest idea of the horror and the magnificence of the scene. One report was as follows: "There is not water deep enough between the islands for a vessel to pass through without danger of splitting on the rocks, which happens even in the calmest weather. The tide comes in rapidly and noisily, and when it goes down roars like the loudest waterfall. The eddies and whirlpools are so numerous and deep that if a ship is once caught in them it is carried to the bottom and there beaten to pieces against the rocks, the fragments of it being later thrown up again.

"The intervals of calm come only at the turn of the tide, and in ordinary weather last only a quarter of an hour. The violence soon comes back again. When the water is most active and its fury increased by a storm, it is dangerous to sail within a mile of it. Ships have been carried away when they have come too close. It happens frequently that whales are caught in it and cannot escape. It is impossible to describe their awful bellowings. A bear was once caught by the stream and carried down, his roars being heard on shore. The bottom must be composed of craggy rocks, for trees carried down come up splintered to pieces. These waters are regulated by the rise and fall of the tide—it being high and low water every six hours. In the year 1645, early one Sunday morning, it raged with such force and noise that the very stones of the houses on the coast fell to the ground."

Looking down from my crag, it appeared to me plain that the largest ships in existence, being caught in that deadly whirlpool, would be like feathers in a hurricane and must disappear entirely and at once. I recalled explanations I had read of this freak of nature, too, none of them satisfactory, all of them not much more than guesses on the part of the writers, for no one could explore those awful depths.

"You have had a good look at the whirl now," said the old man, "and if you will creep around this crag, so as to be sheltered by it and away from the roar of the water, I shall tell you a story that will convince you I ought to know something of the Maelström."

I placed myself as he suggested and prepared to listen.

"My two brothers and I," he began, "once owned a sailing boat in which we used to go fishing among the islands beyond Moskoe, nearly to Vurrgh. There is good fishing in all strong currents of the sea if one has the courage to attempt it. Among all the coastmen, we three were the only ones who made a regular business of going out to the islands, the others heading southward, where there are no risks. The choice spots over here among the rocks, however, yield the finest variety and the greatest abundance. In a single day we often got more fish than the timid ones could scrape together in a week.

"We kept the boat in a cove about five miles up the coast. In fine weather we used to take advantage of the fifteen-minute slack in the whirlpool to cross the main channel far above the pool and then anchor somewhere where the currents were not so violent as elsewhere. Here we remained until nearly time for slack-water again, when we started for home. We never went out on this trip without a steady wind for going and coming, and we seldom made a wrong calculation.

"Twice in six years we had to stay all night at anchor because of a dead calm, which is a rare thing here; and once we were away nearly a week, starving to death, because of a gale which blew up shortly after our arrival and made the channel too rough to venture in. Upon this occasion we would have been driven out to sea, for the whirlpool threw us about so our anchor wouldn't hold, if we had not drifted into one of the many cross-currents—here today and gone tomorrow—which drove us into a sheltered place.

"I could not tell you the twentieth part of the difficulties we met out there; it is a bad spot to be, even in good weather. But we always got by the Moskoe-ström without accident, although my heart has been in my mouth at times when we happened to be a minute or so behind or before the slack. The wind sometimes was not as strong as we thought it at starting, and then we made less speed than we could wish. My eldest brother had a son eighteen years old, and I had two boys of my own. These would have been of great help at such times, but somehow, although we ran the risk ourselves, we hadn't the heart to let the young ones get into danger. After all, it *was* a horrible danger, and that's the truth.

"It is now about three years since what I am going to tell you happened. It was on the tenth of July, a day which the people of this part of the world will never forget, for on it occurred the most terrible hurricane that ever came out of the heavens. And yet all morning, and even until late in the afternoon, there was a gentle and steady breeze from the southwest, while the sun shone so brightly that the oldest seaman among us could not have foreseen what was to follow.

"The three of us—my two brothers and I—had crossed over to the island about two o'clock in the afternoon. Soon we had nearly loaded the boat with fine fish, which, we all remarked, were more plentiful that day than we had ever known them to be. It was just seven *by my watch* when we started for home, so as to get by the worst of the Ström at slack water, which we knew would be at eight.

"A strong wind helped us along, and we proceeded at a great rate, never dreaming of danger, for we saw not the slightest reason to fear it. All at once we were checked by a breeze coming from the land, something that had never happened to us before, and I began to feel a little uneasy without exactly knowing why. We could make no headway at all. I was on the point of proposing a return to the anchorage when we saw the whole horizon behind us covered with a queer, copper-colored cloud, which had come up with amazing speed.

"In the meantime the breeze stopped, and we were completely becalmed, drifting about in every direction. This, however, did not last long enough to give us time to think about it. In less than a minute the storm was upon us; in less than two the sky was entirely overcast. What with this and the driving spray, it became suddenly so dark that we could not see each other in the boat.

"Such a hurricane blew then as could not possibly be described. The oldest seamen in Norway had never experienced anything like it. At the first blast our masts were blown away as if they had been sawed off, the main mast taking with it my younger brother, who had lashed himself to it for safety.

"Our boat was like a feather on the sea. For some moments we lay entirely buried under the waves. How my elder brother escaped drowning I do not know, for

I never had an opportunity to find out. For my part, I threw myself flat on deck, with my hands grasping a ringbolt. It was mere instinct that made me do this sensible thing, for I was much too terrified to think.

"All the time we were under water I held my breath and clung to the bolt. When I could stand it no longer, I raised myself upon my knees, still holding on with my hands, and thus got my head clear. Presently our little boat gave herself a shake, just as a dog does in coming out of the water, and thus rose to some extent to the surface. I was trying to recover my senses and see what could be done when my elder brother grasped my arm. My heart leaped for joy, for I was sure that he was overboard. The next moment my joy was turned to horror. He put his mouth close to my ear and screamed out the dread word, 'Maelström!'

"No one will ever know what my feelings were at that moment. I shook from head to foot. I knew what he meant by that one word well enough. I knew what he wished to make me understand. With the wind that now drove us on, we were bound for the whirlpool, and nothing could save us!

"You understand that on our fishing trips we always went a long way up above the whirlpool and then had to wait and watch carefully for the slack. Now we were driving right toward the center of the danger, and in such a hurricane as this! I knew that we were doomed.

"By this time the first fury of the storm was over, or perhaps we did not feel it so much, as we were driven forward by it. In any case, the sea, which had at first been kept down by the wind, now rose into absolute mountains. A change, too, had come over the sky. In every direction it was still as black as pitch, but nearly overhead there burst out all at once a circular rift of clear sky of a deep bright blue, and through it the full moon blazed with a light that I had never seen before. Everything about us showed up with the greatest distinctness—and what a scene it was!

"I tried to speak to my brother, but the noise had so increased that it was impossible to make him hear a single word, although I screamed at the top of my voice in his ear. Presently he shook his head, looking as pale as death, and held up one of his fingers as if to say *listen!*

"At first I could not make out what he meant—but soon a hideous thought flashed upon me. I took out my watch. It was not going! I studied its face by the moonlight and then burst into tears as I flung it far away into the ocean. *It had run down at seven o'clock! We were behind the time of the slack, and the Maelström was in full fury!*

"So far we had ridden the swells very well; but presently a gigantic sea bore us with it as it rose up—up—up, as if into the sky. I would not have believed that any wave could rise so high. And then we came down with a plunge that made me feel sick and dizzy, as if I were falling from some mountain-top. But while we were up I had thrown a quick glance around—and that was sufficient. I saw our exact position in an instant. The Maelström was about a quarter of a mile ahead—but no more like the everyday whirlpool than this one you see today is like a mill-race. If I had not known where we were and what we had to expect, I should not have recognized the place at all! As it was, I closed my eyes in horror.

"It could not have been more than two minutes afterward when we felt the waves lessen and were surrounded by foam. The boat made a sharp turn and then shot off into a new direction. At the same moment the roaring noise of the water was completely drowned in a kind of shrill shriek. We were now in the belt of surf that always surrounds the whirlpool. I thought, of course, that another moment would plunge us into the abyss, down which we could not see clearly because of the amazing speed with which we were carried along. The boat did not seem to sink into the water at all, but to skim like an air-bubble upon the surface. Her right side was next to the whirlpool, and on the left was the ocean we had left. It stood like a huge wall between us and the horizon.

"Now, when we were in the very jaws of death, I felt more calm than when we were only approaching it. Having made up my mind to hope no more, I got rid of a great deal of my first terror. I suppose it was despair that braced me.

"It may sound like boasting, but I began to think it would be a glorious thing to die in that way. It seemed foolish to think of anything so trifling as my own life, in view of such a wonderful demonstration of God's power. And after a while I found myself curious about the whirlpool itself. I even felt a *wish* to explore its depths, and my principal grief was that I should never be able to tell my old companions on shore about the mysteries I had seen. These were queer ideas to occupy a man's mind. I have often thought since that the turns of the boat around the pool might have made me a little light-headed.

"Then something else happened which made me less afraid; that was the stopping of the wind, which could not reach us where we were now. You saw for yourself that the belt of surf is lower than the general ocean bed, which in our present position towered over us like a high black ridge. If you have ever been at sea in a heavy gale, you know how wind and spray together can blind and strangle you and rob you of the power to think. We were now partly out of this sort of confusion.

"How often we traveled around this belt it is impossible to say. Perhaps an hour we flew rather than floated, getting nearer and nearer to the horrible inner edge of the whirlpool. All this time I had never let go of the ring I had seized. My brother held on to a small, empty water-cask, which had been securely lashed down and was the only thing on deck that had not been swept overboard when the gale first hit us. As we approached the edge of the pit, he let go his hold on this and made for the ring, from which, in the agony of his terror, he tried to force my hands, as it was not large enough for both of us.

"Although I knew he was mad with fear when he did it, I felt deep grief at seeing this. I knew that it could make no difference whether either of us held on at all;

so I let him have the bolt and took his cask. This was, strangely, not hard to do, for the boat flew around steadily enough, and on an even keel, only swaying to and fro. Scarcely had I gained my new position when we gave a lurch and rushed headlong into the abyss. I muttered a prayer to God and thought all was over.

"As I felt the sickening sweep of the descent, I tightened my hold on the barrel and closed my eyes. For some seconds I dared not open them. I expected instant death. But minute after minute passed by. I was still alive. The sense of falling had ceased, and the motion of the vessel was much as it had been before. I took courage and opened my eyes.

"I shall never forget the feelings of horror and admiration with which I looked around me. The boat appeared to be hanging, as if by magic, halfway down upon the inner surface of a funnel, enormous in circumference and vast in depth. Its perfectly smooth sides might have been mistaken for black wool, if it had not been for the speed with which they spun around and for the ghostly glow which came from them. The rays of the full moon streamed in golden glory along the black walls and far down into the depths of the abyss.

"At first I was too much confused to observe anything accurately. When I recovered a little, however, I gazed downward. The rays of the moon seemed to light up the very depths of the funnel, but I could make out nothing distinctly because of the thick mists or sprays sent up from the bottom, where the walls of water must have met. The roar that came from out of that mist I could not possibly describe.

"Our first slide into the abyss itself from the belt of foam above had carried us a great distance down the slope, but our further descent was slower. Round and round we swept in dizzy swings and jerks that sent us sometimes only a few hundred yards, sometimes nearly the complete circuit of the whirlpool. Our progress downward was slow but sure.

"Looking around me, I saw that our boat was not the only object being carried along. Above and below us were parts of ships, building timbers, and trunks of trees, with many smaller articles, such as pieces of house furniture, broken barrels, and boxes. I have already mentioned my unnatural curiosity. It grew upon me as I drew nearer to my doom. I began to watch with strange interest the things floating around us. I guessed at the speed with which they all descended toward the foam below. Perhaps I was losing my mind, but such thoughts came to me. 'This fir tree,' I found myself saying at one time, 'will be the next thing that takes the awful plunge and disappears.' Then I was disappointed to see a Dutch merchant ship overtake it and go down before it. When I had made several mistakes like this, a thought came to me that made me tremble.

"It was not a new terror but the beginning of an exciting *hope*. This came partly from memory and partly from observation. I recalled the great variety of articles that had always drifted to shore after having been drawn down into and cast out of the Maelström. Most of the articles were broken up in a peculiar way; but I remembered distinctly that there were *some* which had not been damaged at all. There must have been some reason for this difference. I concluded that the broken ones had been carried all the way down to the bottom; the others had entered the funnel at a late period of the tide or had descended so slowly that they had not reached the bottom before the tide changed. It seemed possible to me that such articles might be whirled up again to the level of the ocean without being dashed to pieces.

"I noticed other things too. As a general rule, the larger the objects were the more rapidly they descended. If they were round, they went down faster than objects of any other size. If they were cylindrical in shape, they went down slowly.

"Every time we were whirled around we passed a barrel or the mast of a vessel, while many other things which had been on a level with us when we first entered the whirlpool were now high above us.

"I did not hesitate to act. I decided to tie myself securely to the water cask I was holding to, to cut it loose, and to throw myself into the water. I signaled to my brother, pointing to the floating barrels that came near us and trying in every way to make him understand what I was going to do. I thought at last that he understood, but in any case he refused to move from his place. I couldn't reach him. I did not dare to wait. With a bitter struggle I left him to his fate, and, fastening myself to the cask, I jumped into the sea.

"The result was just what I had hoped for. As you see, I did escape. I must bring my story to an end quickly. An hour or so after I had left the boat and when it had descended a great distance below me, I saw it make three or four turns in rapid succession and, bearing my beloved brother with it, plunge headlong at once and forever to destruction. The barrel to which I was fastened had gone only half-way down toward the bottom when a great change took place in the whirlpool. The slope of the sides of the huge funnel became less and less steep. The whirling of the water grew less and less rapid. By degrees the foam disappeared, and the bottom of the gulf seemed to rise gradually. The sky was clear, the wind had gone down, and the full moon was setting brilliantly in the west when I found myself on the surface of the ocean in full view of the shore of the mainland, and above the spot where the Maelström had been. It was the hour of the slack, but the waves were still mountainous from the effects of the hurricane.

"The current carried me down the coast, where a boat picked me up. I was exhausted, and speechless from the memory of the horror I had been through. My rescuers were my daily companions, but they did not recognize me. My hair, which had been black the day before, was as white as you see it now. They say too that the whole expression of my face had altered. I told them my story. They did not believe it. I can scarcely expect you to put any more faith in it than they did."

# *Things Are Not What They Seem*

# WILLIAM WILSON

*"What can I say of it? Of conscience grim,*
*That spectre in my path?"*

LET me call myself, for the present, William Wilson. I need not soil this paper with my real name. That fills too many people with scorn and horror. This is not a story of my later years of misery and unforgivable crime; I want only to tell about the start of my wickedness. Men usually grow bad by degrees; but from me all goodness dropped at once, like a cloak. Now I want to tell what one event brought this evil thing to pass. My death is approaching, and the thought of it has softened me a bit. I long for the sympathy, perhaps even the pity, of my fellow-men. I want them to believe that I am not entirely to blame for what happened. I want them to admit that no one has ever before been tempted to fall as I was. Or have I been living in a dream? And am I dying as the result of one?

My family has always been remarkably imaginative and excitable. In my early youth I showed that I would grow to be the same. As I matured, these traits became stronger. I grew self-willed, changeable, and violent. My weak-minded parents, too much like me in character, could do nothing with me. Their efforts to control me ended with complete failure on their part and of course complete victory on mine. After that I always had my own way, and when I was still a child became complete master of my own actions.

My earliest recollections of school life are connected with a large, rambling Elizabethan house in a misty-looking English village, where all the houses seemed equally ancient. It was a soothing place, that old town. I can still feel the coolness of its shady streets, smell the fragrance of its flowers, and hear the deep notes of the church bell as it struck the hours.

The house was old and irregular, with extensive grounds, surrounded by a high and solid brick wall. This was our entire world; we saw beyond it only three times a week. Every Saturday afternoon, attended by two tutors, we were permitted to take walks through neighboring fields. Twice each Sunday we were paraded in the same formal manner to the morning and evening services in the one church in the village.

The principal of our school was the pastor of this

church. I used to wonder how he could be so solemn, so dignified, and so impressive in church and so sour and strict in the school room.

Within the school enclosure and at the rear of the house was the playground. It was level and covered with fine hard gravel. There were no trees or benches or anything similar on it. In front of the house was a lawn planted with shrubs. We passed along this only on rare occasions—our arrival at the school or final departure from it, or perhaps when a parent or friend called to take us home for Christmas or for the summer vacation.

The quaint old house was a palace of enchantment to me during the five years I spent there. There were many passageways, winding in and out, with rooms opening from them. It was hard to tell the difference between its two stories, so much alike were they. The rooms were on various levels, as they so often are in old, old houses—so that one ascended or descended two or three steps when passing from one room to the next. Eighteen or twenty other students in addition to myself occupied rooms in one wing of the building.

The schoolroom was the largest in the house. To a little boy it seemed the largest in the world. It was long and narrow and had pointed windows and a low oak ceiling. Our principal, the Reverend Doctor Bransby, had his office in a small square room opening off the schoolroom. The teacher of English and mathematics and the teacher of classical subjects had offices, too, far less important to us than that of the principal, but still places to be feared. The rows of benches and desks were black with age and carved by the knives of generations of students with initials, names, and weird figures. A huge bucket of water stood at one end of the room and a clock at the other.

There seems little to remember when I look back upon those days—only the morning's awakening, recitations, the periodical half-holidays, and the playground with its pleasures and its battles. All these made up at the time a life of interest and variety. The years I spent there did not seem dull to me, though looking back on them I find little of importance to mark the days.

Because of my enthusiasm and self-will, I was soon a leader among the boys—with a single exception. Another scholar there had the same name as mine, a circumstance not too surprising since mine was very ordinary. Of course William Wilson is not my real name. My namesake alone of those who were in "our set" competed with me in studies, in class, and in activities on the playground. In addition he refused to agree with my ideas or to follow my orders.

Wilson's independence embarrassed me greatly because I secretly feared him and believed in my heart that he was really a bit above me. Yet my companions seemed not even to suspect our rivalry. He was not ambitious to excel, and seemed to aim only to astonish and upset me. There were even times when he acted fond of me, though I suspected that was because he was conceited and looked down on me.

A rumor gradually spread through the school that we were brothers. We had the same name, had entered school on the same day, had many of the same traits; yet we were not even of the same family. If we had been brothers we must have been twins, for I learned that my namesake was born the same day I was, January 19, 1813.

It may seem strange that, in spite of my anxiety over Wilson's rivalry, I could not bring myself to hate him altogether. To be sure, we had a quarrel nearly every day. I was always victor; yet he made me feel that he had really deserved to be. Only a sense of pride on my part and dignity on his own kept us on speaking terms. We would, I think, have been good friends had we not been rivals.

Wilson had only one weakness I could taunt him with; that was his voice, which he could not raise above a very low whisper. In return he had a way of getting back at me. I hated my name and hated to be called by it. When I found a second Wilson at the academy, I felt doubly disgusted with the name. Now a stranger bore it too. It would be constantly repeated. His affairs, because of it, would be frequently confused with my own.

This feeling grew stronger as I became more and more aware of our close resemblance to each other. We were not only of the same age but also of the same height. He even copied my clothes, my walk, my general manner. And his singular whisper grew to be the very echo of my voice. This again was apparently noticed by no one but me. I could not understand why the school was unaware of it.

He often interfered with me by giving me advice—not openly, but just hinted at. I received it with a disgust which grew upon me with the years. Yet let me do my rival justice. His sense of right and wrong was far higher than mine. Today I might be a better and a happier man if I had accepted the truths given in those meaning whispers which I thoroughly hated and despised.

As it was, I resented him more and more as time went on. In the first years that we were schoolmates together, I might have learned to be friends with him; but in the latter months I positively hated him. One time he saw this and afterward appeared to avoid me. Once I discovered, or thought I discovered, something that brought to me memories of my earliest infancy. I couldn't shake the idea that I had known him at some period long ago. I mention this only because of what happened just before we left the school.

The huge old house had several large rooms leading into each other, where the greater number of the students slept. There were also many little nooks and corners, as are found in most very old houses, which Dr. Bransby had fitted up as dormitories. Each of these was large enough to hold one person. Wilson occupied one of them. One night about the end of my fifth year at the school, I arose after every one had gone to sleep. Lamp in hand, I went through a wilderness of narrow passages from my own room to that of my rival. I had long been planning a practical joke on him and resolved to accomplish it now. Having reached his room, I noiselessly entered, leaving the lamp, with a shade over it, on the outside. I advanced a step and listened to his regular breathing. Assured of his being asleep, I returned for the light; with it I again approached the bed, letting its bright rays fall upon his face. I looked—and a feeling of horror crept upon me. Were these the features of William Wilson? What was there about them to upset me in this manner? He did not look like this in his waking hours. I remembered that he had the same name, the same figure as mine, that he had arrived at the academy the same day I had! And then his imitation of my walk, my voice, my habits, and my manner! Was it possible that what I saw now was the result of this constant imitation? I was looking directly into my own face! With a shudder I put out the lamp, passed quietly from the room, and soon left the school, never to return again.

After several months of idleness I became a student at Eton. Even in that short time I began to forget what had happened and to think I had imagined the whole thing. The life I started at once to lead at Eton put all serious things out of my mind anyway. I will not go into detail here about all the forms of vice with which I occupied my time, in some way escaping the notice of the school authorities. One night, after three years there, I invited a small group of my companions to a wild celebration in my rooms. We met at a late hour, for we intended to keep on until morning. Wine flowed freely until the gray dawn appeared and our party had reached its height. Flushed with the excitement of cards and drink, I was proposing a toast filled with profanity when a servant appeared to tell me that a person apparently in great haste wanted to speak to me in the hall. I was rather delighted than surprised. I staggered to the entrance-way of the building. There was no light in it except the first feeble rays of morning. As I entered I became aware of a youth about my height wearing the same kind of clothes I had on at the time. I could not see his face. He stepped up to me and, seizing my arm, whispered the words, "William Wilson!" in my ear.

I grew perfectly sober in an instant. Something in the manner of the stranger filled me with amazement; but it was not this that had moved me so. It was his low, solemn warning to me. Above all it was the tone of those few whispered syllables. They brought back a thousand memories to me. They made me see all I was, all I had become. Before I could come to my senses he was gone.

This event did not have a very lasting effect on me. For some weeks I thought about it. Of course I was sure my strange visitor had been the companion of my early school days. But who and what was this Wilson? Where did he come from? What was his purpose? I could come to no conclusion about this. All I could find out was that he had left Dr. Bransby's the same day I had.

In a short time I had stopped thinking about it, for I was planning to leave for Oxford. There I soon went, furnished by my vain parents with money enough to live in as great luxury as did the heirs of the wealthiest noblemen in Great Britain. My celebrations started at once. There was no limit to my extravagance and to my sins. All forms of dissipation became familiar to me. It hardly seems possible that I learned all the tricks of a professional gambler, but such was the case. In this way I started to increase my already enormous income at the expense of my weak-minded college mates. No one suspected me of cheating; my own wealth would have made that seem impossible. Besides, William Wilson, the gay, frank, generous William Wilson would never do a thing like that! His vices were only the follies of youth! He would never stoop to anything so low!

For two years I had been successful in this way when a young nobleman, Glendinning, came to the university. He was immensely wealthy. I found him very dull in intellect and so picked him out as my victim. I played with him frequently, letting him often win, so that he would fall completely into my trap. At length, when I had worked out my plans, I met him in the rooms of a mutual friend, Mr. Preston, who did not realize my purpose. To avoid suspicion I had invited eight or ten others and did not let anyone guess that playing cards was the main purpose of the party.

We had celebrated far into the night before I managed to have Glendinning as my opponent. The game, too, was my favorite écarté. The rest of the company were so interested in our playing that they had given up their own cards and were standing around us, looking on eagerly. I had begun to urge Glendinning to drink heavily. Now he shuffled and dealt with a wild nervousness for which the drink was only partly responsible. In a very short time he owed me a large amount of money. Then after a long drink of wine he did exactly what I had been expecting—he proposed to double our extravagant stakes. I pretended to think it a bad idea. Only after he became angry did I consent. The result proved how entirely he had fallen into my trap. In less than an hour he owed me four times as much as he had owed me at the end of the first game.

For some time he had been growing paler and paler. Now he was deathly white. I was astonished. I had heard that Glendinning was immensely wealthy. The sums which he had already lost, though they were huge, should not have affected him so violently. I thought it must be the wine and was about to suggest that we stop the game. Suddenly an expression of complete despair on his part made me understand that I had ruined him completely.

For some minutes there was a deep silence in the room. Everyone was embarrassed over the pitiful condition of my victim. I could not but blush because of the glances of scorn and reproach cast at me by the better men among the guests. I was even a bit relieved at the extraordinary interruption that came now. The heavy folding-doors of the apartment were all at once thrown wide open with a rush that put out as if by magic every candle in the room. Their dying light showed us a stranger, about my own height, closely wrapped in a cloak. When it became entirely dark, we could only feel that he was standing in our midst. Before any of us could recover from surprise, we heard the voice of the intruder.

"Gentlemen," he said, in a never-to-be-forgotten *whisper*, "I will not apologize for my behavior, for I am only fulfilling a duty. You probably don't know the true character of the person who has just won a large sum of money from Lord Glendinning. I will let you know at once. Examine the inner lining of the cuff of his left sleeve, and the big pockets of his embroidered house coat."

While he spoke there was complete stillness in the room. When he had stopped, he left at once as abruptly as he had entered. How can I describe my feelings? I had little time for thought. Many hands seized me roughly, and lights were brought at once. I was searched. Marked cards were found in my sleeve linings and in my pockets. The silent contempt of the company was hard to bear.

"Mr. Wilson," said our host, stooping to pick up an expensive fur coat, "this is your property. I suppose it isn't necessary to look in it for any further evidence of your skill. We have had quite enough. I hope you will see the necessity for leaving Oxford. In any case I want you to leave my rooms at once."

Ashamed as I was, I would probably have resisted violently if my attention had not been caught by something startling. The cloak which I had worn was made of a rare type of expensive fur. I had designed it myself. When Mr. Preston handed me the one he had picked up, I was terrified to see my own coat already hanging on my arm. The one he had given me was its exact duplicate to the smallest detail. I remembered that the strange being who had exposed my guilt had been muffled in a cloak. Keeping some presence of mind, I took the one offered me by Preston and with both departed. Next morning before dawn I had left Oxford and had fled to the continent in a perfect agony of horror and shame.

I fled in vain. My evil fate pursued me. Scarcely had I arrived in Paris when I realized that Wilson was continuing his interest in my affairs. Years flew by. I felt no relief. In Rome he stepped between me and my ambition. He appeared in Vienna, in Berlin, and in Moscow. I fled from him to the very end of the earth. I fled in vain.

Again and again I would ask myself, "Who is he? Where did he come from? What is his purpose?" But I found no answer. I could only guess at the fact that he had come each time when I was about to commit some wicked act and each time had kept me from its completion.

Never had I seen his face, though he was always dressed exactly like me. This was surely folly on his part. How could I fail to recognize him as the William Wilson of my school days, my hated namesake and rival at Dr. Bransby's? And now he came to ruin my ambition at Rome, my revenge in Paris, my passionate love in Naples, my greed in Egypt, just as he had warned me at Eton and had destroyed my honor at Oxford.

All along I had given in to his will. His noble character and his wisdom had made me realize my own weakness and helplessness. Finally I gave myself up entirely to wine, and it made me more and more impatient of control. I began to resist Wilson. Did I only imagine that the stronger I became the weaker he grew? I now began to have a burning hope and a desperate resolution to be no longer a slave to him.

At Rome in Carnival time[1] I attended a masquerade at the palace of the Duke Di Broglio. I had been drinking more freely than usual, and the close atmosphere of the room irritated me beyond endurance. The difficulty, too, of forcing my way among the crowd ruffled my temper even more. I was seeking, with evil purpose, the young and beautiful wife of the aged Di Broglio. She had told me beforehand what she would be wearing, and I had caught a glimpse of her in the crowd.

Suddenly I felt a light hand on my shoulder and heard that ever-remembered whisper in my ear. I turned in a frenzy of wrath and seized the owner of the voice by the collar. He was clothed, as I had expected, in a costume exactly like mine, a Spanish cloak of blue velvet, with a crimson belt, holding a rapier, about the waist. A mask of black silk entirely covered his face.

"Scoundrel!" I said, in a voice hoarse with rage. "Accursed villain! You shall not follow me until death. Ap-

[1] Carnival time—January 17 until Ash Wednesday. To celebrate this period just before Lent, pageants, masquerades, etc., are held throughout Italy.

proach me now and I shall stab you where you stand."
I rushed away from the ballroom to a small reception hall, dragging him with me as I went.

When we had entered, I pushed him furiously away from me. He staggered against the wall, while I closed the door with an oath and commanded him to draw out his weapon. He hesitated only an instant and then with a slight sigh began to defend himself.

The contest was brief. I was frantic with excitement and felt full of power. In a few seconds I had forced him to the wall and, getting him at my mercy, plunged my sword with brutal fierceness again and again through his chest.

At that instant someone tried to open the door. I hastened to prevent this and then returned to my dying antagonist. How can I express the horror which filled me at the sight before me? In the moment when my eyes had been turned away from the room a great change had come about in it. A large mirror now stood where none had been visible before. As I stepped up to it in terror, what seemed to be my own reflection but with features pale and dabbled with blood advanced to meet me with a feeble and tottering gait.

It seemed to be my own figure, but was not. It was my foe—it was Wilson who stood up before me in the agony of his death. His mask and cloak lay where he had thrown them upon the floor. There was nothing at all about him that was not in every detail like me.

It was Wilson, but he spoke no longer in a whisper, and I could have imagined I was speaking as he said,

"You have conquered, and I yield. Yet henceforward thou art also dead—dead to the world, to Heaven, and to Hope! In me thou didst exist, and in my death see how utterly thou hast murdered thyself."

Now, years afterward, I write my record, leaving out my later years of misery and of unpardonable crime. Men usually grow bad by degrees; but from me all goodness dropped at once, like a cloak. Now you have heard what event brought this evil thing to pass. It was my murder of William Wilson—of the goodness in my nature, of the conscience and the desire for nobility which lies deep in the heart of us all.

# *A Sidelight on History*

# THE PIT AND THE PENDULUM

I WAS sick—sick unto death with the long agony of my trial at the Inquisition,[1] and when they at length unbound me and I was permitted to sit up, I felt that I was losing consciousness. The sentence—the dread sentence of death—was the last thing which reached my ears clearly. After that, the sound of the questioning voices seemed blurred to one dreamy hum, like that of a mill wheel. For only a brief period I heard this, and then no more.

Yet for a while I could see. I saw the lips of the black-robed judges. They appeared to me white, whiter than

[1] Inquisition—A religious campaign conducted in the Middle Ages to punish those who were not followers of the Church.

the paper upon which I write these words, and thin from the fierceness of their resolution and their contempt of human torture. Then I saw them form the syllables of my name and pronounce my doom. I saw, too, for a few minutes of delirious horror, the soft waving of the black draperies which covered the walls of the room. And then my eyes fell upon the seven tall candles on the table. At first they seemed like white slender angels who would save me; but then a deadly sickness came over my spirit. The angel forms became meaningless ghosts with heads of flame, and I saw that from them there would be no help.

And then there stole into my mind the thought of what sweet rest there must be in the grave. Scarcely had I begun to feel this when the judges vanished as if by magic before me, the flames of the candles went out utterly, black darkness came upon me, and all sensation ceased. Then came silence and stillness and night.

I had fainted, but still cannot say that all consciousness was lost. Looking back upon it, struggling earnestly since then for some remembrance of those hours, there have been brief periods when vague memories have come back to me. These shadows of memory tell of tall figures that lifted and carried me down, down, down, still down—until hideous dizziness oppressed me at the mere thought of the endlessness of the descent. Then came a sense of sudden stillness, as if those who carried me had paused from the weariness of their toil. After this I recall flatness and dampness. Then all is lost in forgetfulness.

Very suddenly there came back to me motion and sound—the rapid motion of my heart, and in my ears the sound of its beating. Then came a pause in which all was blank. Then, very suddenly, *thought* and shuddering terror followed, and an earnest attempt to understand my circumstances. Then came a rushing return of memory and a successful effort to move. And now a full memory of the trial, of the judges, of the black draperies, of my sentence, of the swoon was with me.

So far, I had not opened my eyes. I felt that I lay upon my back unbound. I reached out my hand, and it fell heavily upon something damp and hard. I left it there for several moments, trying to recall where I could be. I longed to open my eyes, yet dared not do so. I dreaded my first glimpse at objects around me. It was not that I was afraid to look at horrible things, but that I was terrified lest there be *nothing* to see. At length, with wild desperation, I quickly opened my eyes. My worst thoughts, then, were confirmed. I was in total darkness.

I struggled for breath. The darkness seemed to stifle me. The atmosphere was unbearably close. I lay still quietly and tried to use my reason. I recalled the trial and tried to figure out my real condition. Sentence had been pronounced on me. Apparently a long time had passed since that sentence. Those condemned to death, I knew, perished at public executions, and one of them had been conducted on the very night of my trial. Had I been thrown into this dungeon to await the next one, which would not take place for many months? This I at once saw could not be. Victims had been in immediate demand. Moreover, the dungeon where I had been imprisoned, as well as all the condemned cells at Toledo, had stone floors and at least some light.

A fearful idea now suddenly seized me, and for a brief period I lost consciousness again. Upon recovering I at once started to my feet, trembling all over. I thrust my arms wildly above and around me in all directions. I felt nothing, yet dreaded to move a step lest I should find myself enclosed within the walls of a *tomb*. The agony of suspense grew unbearable. I cautiously moved forward with my arms extended and my eyes straining to catch some feeble ray of light. I proceeded many paces; but still all was blackness and vacancy. I breathed more freely. I had not, then, been buried alive.

As I still continued to step cautiously forward, there came to my recollection a thousand rumors of the horrors of the Toledo dungeons, some too ghastly to repeat. Had I been left to die of starvation in this dark place? Or what fate, perhaps even more fearful, awaited me? I knew my judges well enough to be sure that my death would be one of more than usual horror. When I would die and how were all that occupied my thoughts now.

My outstretched hands at length touched a wall, seemingly of stone, very smooth, slimy, and cold. I followed along it, stepping carefully. This process, however, would not enable me to figure the size of my dungeon. I might travel all around it without recognizing the point at which I had started, so uniform was the wall. I therefore sought the knife which I had had in my pocket when they led me to my trial, but it was gone; my clothes had been exchanged for a robe of coarse serge. I had thought of forcing the blade into some crack in the masonry, and so recognizing the point at which I had started. This difficulty was, however, trifling. I tore a part of the hem from the robe, and placed the piece at full length and at right angles to the wall. In groping my way around the prison, I could not fail to come upon this rag when I had completed the circuit. So, at least, I thought. I had not counted on the size of the dungeon or on my own weakness. The ground was moist and slippery. I staggered on for some time, then stumbled and fell. I lay still, exhausted, until sleep overcame me.

Upon awaking, I found beside me a loaf of bread and a pitcher of water. Too exhausted to question them, I ate and drank eagerly. Shortly afterward I continued my tour around the prison and at last came upon the piece of serge. I had counted in all a hundred paces; admitting two paces to the yard, I figured the dungeon to be fifty yards in circuit. I could form no guess as to its shape because of the many angles I had met in my way around it.

I had little motive—certainly no hope—in these investigations; but a vague curiosity led me to continue them. Leaving the wall, I decided to cross the enclosure. At first I proceeded with extreme caution, for the floor, although seeming to be of solid material, was dangerously slimy. At length I took courage and resolved to cross it in as direct a line as possible. I had advanced some ten or twelve paces in this manner, when the torn hem of my robe became entangled between my legs. I stepped on it and fell violently on my face.

In the confusion of my fall, I did not at once notice a startling circumstance which, a few seconds afterward and while I still lay prostrate, attracted my attention. It was this: my chin rested on the floor of the prison, but my lips and the upper part of my head touched nothing. At the same time my forehead was wet with a clammy vapor, and the peculiar smell of rotting leaves was in my nose. I reached out—and shuddered to find that I had fallen at the very brink of a circular pit. Groping about the masonry just below the edge, I dislodged a small piece and let it fall into the opening. For many seconds I listened to its echoes as it dashed against the sides of the chasm in its descent. At length it plunged into the water below. At the same moment there came the sound of a quick opening and closing of a door overhead, while a faint gleam of light flashed through the gloom and as suddenly faded away.

I saw clearly the doom which had been prepared for me and congratulated myself on the accident by which I had escaped. Another step before my fall, and the world would have seen me no more. For the victims of the Inquisition there was a choice of death with its dire *physical* agonies or death with its most hideous *mental* horrors. I had been reserved for the latter. By long suffering my nerves had been shattered until I trembled at the sound of my own voice and had become a fitting subject for the kind of torture which awaited me.

Shaking in every limb, I groped my way back to the wall, resolving to die there rather than risk the terror of the pit. In my normal state I might have had courage to end my misery at once by a plunge into the abyss; now I was a coward.

Fear kept me awake for many long hours, but at length I again fell asleep. Upon awaking I found at my side as before a loaf and a pitcher of water. A burning thirst attacked me, and I drank the water greedily. It must have been drugged, for I became drowsy at once. A sleep like that of death came upon me. How long it lasted I do not know; but, when I at last opened my eyes, I could see the objects around me.

I had been greatly mistaken in the size of my prison, which was not even twenty-five yards around. I had been deceived, too, as to the shape of the enclosure. In feeling my way I had found many angles and thus concluded that it was very irregular; the angles, however, were simply niches at odd intervals. The general shape of the prison was square. What I had taken for masonry seemed now to be iron or some other metal. The entire surface of this enclosure was painted in hideous and repulsive devices. There were figures of fiends, of skeleton forms, of other fearful images. Their outlines were distinct, but the color seemed faded and blurred as from the dampness. The floor was of stone. In the center was the circular pit from which I had escaped.

As I slept, I had been moved. I now lay upon my back full length on a low framework of wood, to which I was securely bound by a long strap, which was passed several times around my limbs and body, leaving free only my head and, to a limited extent, my left arm. With this, by dint of much stretching, I could supply myself with food from an earthen dish which lay beside me on the floor. I saw, to my horror, that the pitcher had been removed. I had now an unbearable thirst, which my persecutors seemed to be encouraging by giving me highly seasoned food.

Looking upward, I examined the ceiling of my prison, which was thirty or forty feet above me. A curious thing there drew my whole attention. It was the painted figure of Father Time, as he is commonly pictured, except that in place of a scythe he held what looked to be a huge pendulum such as we see on antique clocks. Something about this caused me to look at it more attentively. While I gazed directly up at it (for it was immediately above me) I fancied that I saw it moving. An instant afterward I was sure of it. Its sweep was short and, of course, slow. I watched it for some minutes, more in wonder than in fear. Tired at last, I turned my eyes on the other objects in the cell.

A slight noise attracted my attention, and, looking at the floor, I saw several enormous rats running around. While I watched, they came up out of the well, which lay just to my right, in troops, hurriedly, with hungry eyes, attracted by the smell of the meat. I scared them away with difficulty.

Half an hour or perhaps an hour later I again looked up to the ceiling. What I saw confused and amazed me. The sweep of the pendulum had increased in extent by nearly a yard. Its speed was consequently much greater. But what chiefly disturbed me was that it had noticeably *descended.* I now observed with horror that the bottom edge of it was formed of a crescent of glittering steel about a foot in length from end to end. The edge of it was evidently as sharp and heavy. It was attached to a rod of brass, and the whole thing *hissed* as it swung through the air.

I could no longer doubt the doom prepared for me. I had avoided a plunge into the pit by a mere accident. Having failed to fall, I was not to be thrown into it. A different destruction now awaited me. The pendulum was to descend gradually upon me, until it cut me in half.

I need not tell of the long, long hours of terror more than human during which I counted the swingings of the pendulum. Inch by inch, line by line, with a descent only noticeable at intervals that seemed ages, down and still down it came. Days passed; it might have been many days that passed before it swept so closely over me as to fan me. I prayed constantly for its more speedy descent. I grew frantic and struggled to force myself up against the fearful knife and thus put an end to my torture.

Then came another interval of unconsciousness. When I came to life I noticed that the pendulum was no closer; I knew that the demons who had imprisoned me were watching me and had stopped its motion until I was awake again. Upon my recovery I felt sick and weak, and even, in spite of my agonies, hungry.

With painful effort I stretched out my left arm for the small remnant of food that the rats had spared me. As I put it to my lips, a half-formed ray of hope seized me. Yet what business had I with hope? The feeling left at once.

The vibration of the pendulum was at right angles to my length. I saw that it was to cross the region of my heart, first fraying the serge of my robe. It would then return and repeat its operation again and again. In spite of its wide sweep—some thirty feet or more—this was all it could accomplish for several minutes. I thought about this again and again, as though by thinking I could stop the descent of the blade.

Down, steadily down it crept. It vibrated within three inches of my chest. I struggled violently, furiously, to free my left arm, which was unbound only from the elbow to the hand. If I could have broken the fastenings above the elbow, I would have seized and attempted to stop the pendulum. I might as well have attempted to stop an avalanche.

Down, still down it came. I gasped and struggled at each vibration. I shrank at every sweep. I quivered in every nerve to think how slight a sinking of the machinery would place the axe directly upon me. And still my earlier hope, even now, returned to me.

I saw that ten or twelve vibrations would bring the steel in actual contact with my robe. With this observation and with all the calmness of despair, for the first time I really *thought*. It now occurred to me that the strap or bandage by which I was tied was unique. It was all in one piece. The first stroke of the blade across any section of the band would so cut it that it might be unwound by my left hand. But was it likely that the torturers had not foreseen and provided for this possibility? Dreading to find my dim and final hope in vain, I lifted my head so as to get a clear view of my breast, where the knife was aiming. The bands covered my limbs and body closely in all directions—except on the spot where the blade would descend and cut me.

Scarcely had I put my head down again than there flashed into my mind the unformed half of the idea for my deliverance which I have referred to before. The whole plan was now present—feeble but still complete. I proceeded at once with the energy of despair to attempt to carry it out.

For many hours rats had been swarming all around me. They were wild, bold, starving. They seemed to be waiting to make me their prey. "To what food," I thought, "had they become accustomed in the well?" In spite of my efforts to prevent them, by waving my hand constantly, they had devoured all but a small remnant of the contents of my dish. In their hunger they had frequently fastened their sharp teeth in my fingers. With the particles of the greasy and spicy food which now remained, I thoroughly rubbed my bandage wherever I could reach it. Then, raising my hand from the floor, I remained breathlessly still.

At first the starved animals were startled by this change in my movement. But this was only for a moment. I had not counted in vain on their hunger. Seeing that I remained without motion, one or two leaped upon the framework on which I lay and smelt my bands. This seemed the signal for a general rush. From the well they hurried out in fresh troops. They leaped in hundreds upon my person. The movement of the pendulum disturbed them not at all. Avoiding its strokes, they busied themselves with the food-smeared bandage. They pressed, they swarmed over me. They crawled upon my throat. I was half stifled by their pressure. Disgust beyond words overwhelmed me and chilled my heart. Yet in one minute I felt that the struggle would be over. I could plainly feel the loosening of the bandage; I knew that in more than one place it must be eaten apart. With resolution I lay *still.*

I was not wrong in my figuring. I had not suffered in vain. At length I felt that I was *free.* The bandage hung in ribbons from my body. But the stroke of the pendulum already pressed upon my chest. It had cut into the serge of my robe. It had cut through the linen beneath. Twice again it swung, and a sharp sense of pain shot through every nerve. But the moment of escape had arrived. At a wave of my hand my deliverers hurried away. With a steady movement—cautions, sidelong, shrinking, and slow, I slid out from the bandages and beyond the reach of the knife. For the moment, at least, I was *free.* Free—but still in the grasp of the Inquisition! I had scarcely stepped from my wooden bed of horror upon the stone floor of the prison when the motion of the hellish machine ceased, and I saw it drawn, by some invisible force, through the ceiling.

This was a lesson that I took desperately to heart. Free! I had escaped death in one form of agony to be delivered to worse than death in some other.

With that thought I looked nervously around on the walls of iron that hemmed me in. Something unusual, some change which at first I could not detect, had taken place in the dungeon. For many minutes I busied myself in vain guesses. During this time I became aware for the first time of the origin of the light which brightened the cell. It came from a crack, about half an inch in width, extending entirely around the prison at the bottom of the walls, which were completely separated from the floor. I tried, but of course in vain, to look through the crack.

As I arose from this attempt, I began to understand the mystery of the change in the room. I had already observed that, although the outlines of the figures upon the walls were distinct, the colors seemed blurred and dim. These colors were now assuming a startling and most intense brilliancy that gave to the ghostly and fiendish figures an appearance that might have destroyed even firmer nerves than mine. I saw demon eyes in a thousand directions where none had been visible before. I saw fiends grinning at me.

Then there came to my nostrils the smell of heated iron. A suffocating odor spread through the prison. A deeper glow showed each moment in the eyes that glared at my agonies. A deeper crimson color spread over the pictured horrors. I panted! I gasped for breath! There could be no doubt of the purpose of my tormentors! I shrank from the glowing metal to the center of the cell. Amid the thoughts of the fiery doom prepared for me, the idea of the coolness of the well came. I rushed to its edge. The glare from the heated roof illumined its darkest portions. For a moment my mind refused to believe what I saw therein. I felt that any fate would be better than that of other victims, who had plunged in. With a shriek I rushed from the edge and buried my face in my hands, weeping bitterly.

The heat rapidly increased. When I looked up once again, I saw that there had been a second change in the cell. The room had been square. Its size and form were being gradually altered. With a low rumbling or moaning its burning walls were now coming closer and closer to me. I saw that it was the design of my persecutor to force me into the pit. Could I resist the heat? Could I withstand the pressure of the walls upon me? Smaller and smaller grew the space in which I was confined. Its center came just over the yawning gulf. I shrank back, but the closing walls pressed me onward.

At length for my burned and writhing body there was no longer an inch of foothold on the firm floor of the prison. I struggled no more. I gave one loud, long, and final scream of despair. I tottered to the edge of the pit. I turned my eyes away.

There came a hum of human voices! There was a loud blast of many trumpets! There was a harsh grating as of thunder. The fiery walls rushed back. An outstretched arm caught mine as I fell fainting into the pit. The French army had entered the city. I was saved.

# "IN SEARCH OF ELDORADO"

## EDGAR ALLAN POE: HIS LIFE

THE MAN who wrote the stories which you have just finished spent all his life searching. The Eldorado—the Land of Gold—which he sought was not a place of riches or power; his quest was for a place of happiness, security, and peace. Seeking these things, he was granted instead the gifts of vivid imagination, weird fancy, colorful words —all of them products of the strange and restless life he led.

For the life of Edgar Allan Poe was in a great many respects as remarkable as are the tales in this book. He was in truth a "man of mystery." So many stories about him have come down to us through the years that it is not always easy to tell just which are true and which were influenced by the imaginations of people who knew him. Yet we know enough facts about him to help us see why he thought and wrote as he did.

His life is a study in contrasts. He knew most of the great writers of his day, Lowell and Longfellow, for instance; yet few people ever fully appreciated him or his work during his lifetime. He made fortunes for the owners of magazines which he edited, but lived most of his life in terrible poverty. His first volume of poems, published when he was only eighteen, attracted almost no notice, though now each one of the five copies in existence is worth a fortune to its owner and one is in the British Museum. An original manuscript of his poem, "The Raven," recently sold for $10,000. Poe received ten dollars for it. He left both the University of Virginia and the United States Military Academy at West Point in disgrace. Now each school has a memorial to him. He was handsome, talented, and popular, but so unhappy that he often wished himself dead and once tried to commit suicide.

His character is a hard one to understand. He was a genius. For him that meant not only brilliance of mind, but a nervous system so delicate and sensitive that harsh experiences and unsympathetic treatment brought torture and despair to him. He could face the world and manage his life when all went well, but when misfortunes came he could not bear them. You have probably heard that he drank too much and took drugs at times. He was not a drunkard, however. Many people who came in contact with him knew him only as sober and hard-working. But sometimes, when the strain of living was too great, the temptation to drink was too strong. Because his health was never good and his heart always weak, he was very much affected by even a small amount of stimulant. That led to misfortunes during his life and to his final downfall.

Poe's parents were actors. His beautiful and talented mother, Mrs. Elizabeth Arnold Poe, who was born in England, came from a family of actors. His father, David Poe, a Baltimore man who had been trained as a lawyer, offended his family by marrying an actress and going on the stage. Poe was born in Boston, Massachusetts, on January 19, 1809. He was the second of three children, having an older brother William and a younger sister Rosalie.

No one knows very much about the first few years of Poe's life, until his mother came to Richmond, Virginia, in August, 1811, to act in a play. She was then, at twenty-four years of age, dying of tuberculosis, but was forced to go on with her acting to support herself and her two children. Poe's father had recently died of tuberculosis, and his older brother William had been adopted by the Poe family in Baltimore. Those last days of his mother's life must have made an impression on Edgar, young as he was.

As his mother grew too ill to appear in plays, the fashionable Richmond ladies became interested in the poor widow and her two children and called on her in her miserable room over a milliner's shop. Her theatrical company gave benefit performances for her to make her last days a little easier. She died on December 8, 1811, and was buried in the churchyard of St. John's—the same church in which Patrick Henry had made his famous speech, several years before.

Even an average child almost three years old would be bewildered and heartbroken at the loss of his mother. You can imagine, then, what effect it must have had on Edgar. He and Rosalie were with her all through their mother's last illness. They probably were at her bedside when she died. It is possible that the feeling of terrible fear and loneliness from which Poe suffered most of his life started with his final separation from his young mother.

Among the Richmond ladies who had helped the poor little family were two of importance to our story. One of them, Mrs. William Mackenzie, adopted Rosalie, a beau-

ST. JOHN'S CHURCHYARD

HERE IS BURIED THE MOTHER OF EDGAR ALLAN POE

tiful little girl, who was, however, never very bright and who remained throughout her life not much older than a child in mind. Her home was a happy one.

Mrs. John Allan, who lived near the Poes, took Edgar into her home. She had no children and adored the boy right from the start. Perhaps she adored him too much, for she petted and spoiled him during his childhood. He in turn clung to her for love and protection in his motherless world. John Allan was a Scotch merchant, a stern and cold man, who could never forget that Poe was the son of actors, a class of people looked down upon in those days. He would never legally adopt him. Still, he seemed fond of the boy and probably did not understand that this attitude would give Edgar a feeling of inferiority and insecurity. Poe's father's people in Baltimore wanted him badly, but the Allans would not give him up. So he was raised as one of the family and took the name of Edgar Allan, only adding Poe when he was in his teens.

At this time he was a handsome boy with dark curls and brilliant eyes. He was always dressed elaborately. He had a wonderful memory and could dance and recite. The Allans often had him perform for their guests. He had all the pocket money he wanted and a pony to ride. His life then gave promise of being a perfectly normal and happy one.

John Allan's company sold tobacco, grain, and liquors, and traded in horses and slaves. Ships delivered cargoes to it and planters' wagons loaded up for trips to the West. The boy, who was always welcome at the store, must have met many people who gave him ideas about which he was to write later. His home, like all the wealthy ones in the South at the time, was staffed by slaves. From them he learned of spooks and goblins, of corpses and burials. You know how much use he made of them in his tales.

In 1815, when Poe was seven, the Allan family went to Scotland, the land of Mr. Allan's birth. That thirty-six-day trip gave Edgar his first intimate knowledge of boats and the sea. For a time they settled in Ayrshire, and Poe attended the village school. In the spring of 1817 he was sent to a private school in England whose principal was John Bransby. You have read about him and his school in "William Wilson", which is partly about Poe himself. He apparently began here to realize that there was a bad side to his nature and that he would have trouble in following the right path. A sense of loneliness and fear often made him miserable. Here, too, he learned to love ancient castles such as the ones he has described in "The Fall of the House of Usher" and "Ligeia". He began to write poetry even in these early days and to take an intense interest in his studies.

In 1820, the family returned to Richmond. Poe was then eleven. Life for the next six years was apparently normal, and Poe's physical development was rapid—in fact, he once startled his friends by swimming for six miles, a great feat of strength for one his age. He was somewhat of a hero among his friends and a good student in the private school he attended. Yet he was often moody and reckless. Nightmares which were to trouble him the rest of his life started at this time. He went for long walks alone at night. When he continued writing poetry, the practical, common sense Mr. Allan was not pleased. He reminded the boy of his heritage and his position in the household as only a dependent. And the "society" people of Richmond looked down on Edgar just a little.

Several of his experiences during these six years stand out as important. In the autumn of 1824, Lafayette came to Richmond. Poe was then a lieutenant in the Junior Home Guards and was appointed as the great general's bodyguard. His Baltimore grandfather, David Poe, had served with credit in the Revolution, had been given the courtesy title of "General", and had been a friend of both Washington and Lafayette. Poe must have been given special attention because of his grandfather. The whole experience influenced him later toward a military career.

When he was sixteen he met the mother of his friend, Bob Stanard, Mrs. Jane Stith Stanard. She was an intelligent woman, and to her Edgar turned for the understanding and sympathy the Allans did not give him. She listened to his poetry and encouraged him to go on writing. Her influence on the sensitive, moody boy was immense. His first beautiful poem, "To Helen", was written for her. He said afterward that he haunted her grave when she died April, 1824.

Another important relationship was his love affair with a neighbor's fifteen-year-old daughter, Sarah Elmira Royster. She played the piano and he the flute. They walked together in a beautiful garden and became secretly engaged. But neither family approved the match. When Poe went to college their letters were intercepted, and she shortly married a much older man.

In 1825 Allan bought an elaborate new home in which Poe had his own lovely room. In spite of his foster-father's misgivings about him because of his "dreamings", his spells of gloom, and his poetry, Allan still had ambitions for the boy and hired tutors to prepare him for entering the University of Virginia. In February 1826, when the seventeen-year old Poe entered, the University had been open less than a year. It was founded by Thomas Jefferson, who was

THE MEMORIAL GARDEN IN THE REAR OF THE POE SHRINE, RICHMOND, VIRGINIA

still alive in 1826 and who must have been a familiar figure to Poe. It numbered only 177 pupils, most of them rich young men who were there for fun rather than for study. Like so many of his Richmond associates, they looked down on Poe because of his humble birth. His position here was doubly hard, for though he seemed to be the heir of an immensely wealthy man, he really had no safe position in the world. And John Allan, thinking possibly to discourage the extravagant spending habits which he himself had encouraged in the boy, sent almost no money. You can see why a person like Poe would have gotten into difficulties. He gambled to pay his expenses—and lost. He associated with gay young companions—and drank too much. We have seen that drink had a very serious effect on him. Here he discovered for the first time that a little of it would make him feel bold and reckless and important. Soon he had run up a large gambling debt.

Through it all Poe did not neglect his studies. He was so brilliant that without hard study he maintained a high rank in his classes. Much of his time was spent in the library, and much in taking solitary walks in the nearby mountains, where he found material for some of his tales. His cleverness was admired by the other boys, to whom he recited his poems, and he was respected by his teachers. But finally his bills reached Allan, who came to the University at Christmas time of 1826. He refused to pay Poe's debts and withdrew him from the University.

Back in Richmond, life was very unpleasant for Poe. Only the colored servants and Mrs. Allan, who loved him until the end, made life bearable. Finally, in March of 1827, after a terrible quarrel with the man who had assumed responsibility for him and from whom he still expected all the comfort and luxury he had always had, Poe fled from the house without money or extra clothes. Pitiful letters to Mr. Allan brought no reply, but Mrs. Allan sent him money, with which he bought passage for the two-month trip to Boston, the city of his birth.

During his short stay there he met a young printer, Calvin Thomas, who published his first book, "Tamerlane and Other Poems". Though anyone who owns a copy of this now is wealthy, it attracted almost no notice when it came out. Poe, by that time practically starving, enlisted in the Army.

He was a good soldier! Discipline and a regular life helped him, and he advanced steadily in rank until he became a sergeant-major, the highest non-commissioned officer. He was stationed first at Fort Independence in Boston Harbor and then transferred to Fort Moultrie, Sullivan's Island, North Carolina. This is the scene of his most famous story, "The Gold Bug", and here it was that he got the ideas and the background for it. Here, too, he went on writing poetry and making plans for another book. He felt sure he was a man of genius. He would not give up his writing.

After Poe had been in the Army more than a year, he wrote again to Mr. Allan. He wished to get a discharge, so that he could go on with his writing or get an appointment to West Point. At first he had no reply, but Mr. Allan later relented. Mrs. Allan was dying and begged to see the boy who had been a son to her for many years. He was finally sent for, but she was dead before he arrived. Some sort of peace was made with Mr. Allan, however, and plans started for his release from the Army and appointment to West Point. He was discharged on April 15, 1829, at the age of 20, with high praise from his superior officers.

Meanwhile, Poe's relatives in Baltimore, who were later to be so important to him, had featured very little in his life. While he was waiting for his appointment to West Point, he went to stay with his father's people. You remember his grandfather, David Poe, the friend of Lafayette.

You remember Poe's older brother, William, who had been adopted by the Baltimore relatives. He is important in this story for only one thing. He had been in the Navy or the Merchant Marine and told Poe many vivid stories to be added to his store for future use. William died at 25, a drunkard.

In the household in Baltimore was also Poe's aunt, Mrs. Maria Poe Clemm, a widow, who was to be Poe's protector and support for all the rest of his life. She was a motherly woman, always willing to do for others. She was sure that "Eddie", as she called him, was a genius. In spite of the family's poverty, she took him in and regarded him as a son. She always befriended him thereafter whenever he needed her. If there was no money or no food, she went out and begged for it. And, shortly after this, Poe's experience with little or no money and little or no food was to start and to continue until his death.

The final important member of the Baltimore family was Mrs. Clemm's daughter Virginia, Poe's cousin, a lovely child of seven, who adored "Cousin Eddie". Mr. Allan was still refusing to send money, accusing Poe of drinking excessively, which was not true at that time. Poe even walked from Baltimore to Washington to press the West Point appointment. Meanwhile, in a garret of the Baltimore house, he continued with his poetry and finally had his second book, "Al Aaraaf, Tamerlane, and Minor Poems", published. Like the first, it brought him neither money nor fame.

Finally, in June of 1830, when he was twenty-one, the appointment came, and Poe started sadly off. He knew what army life was like, but he had no choice. He must go to West Point or starve. He was in bad health, too. Already the heart trouble which was to bother him the rest of his life had started. His high-strung nature had suffered from his unfortunate experiences. What he needed was peace, solitude, and freedom from financial strain. He always needed these. He never got them.

At West Point, as at the University of Virginia, he was looked down upon by the boys, who knew he had been a "common soldier". Here, too, he passed his courses brilliantly. Here, too, he had no money. Mr. Allan was about to marry again and was losing all interest in him. Poe was older than the other boys and found no friends among them. He was lonely and homesick. As always when the world got too much for him, he began to drink again. He did go on with his poetry though, and the Colonel allowed him to publish another book, for which the boys at the school subscribed the money. Finally, discouraged by the life there and miserable over Mr. Allan's attitude, he wrote his foster-father that he wanted to leave and would get himself court-martialed for neglect of duty unless Mr. Allan would secure his honorable discharge. That was refused, and in February he was dismissed. Aside from one violent interview with him two years later, he never saw Mr. Allan again and was cut off entirely in his will.

He had the Baltimore relatives, especially his aunt, Mrs. Clemm, to fly to for comfort and protection. Poor though they were, he knew they would take him in. But on the way to them he stayed in New York a month or so, ill with ear trouble and a weak heart. At this time the book he had written at West Point was published. Perhaps the beautiful poetry in it comforted his heart a bit. It did not provide him with funds for food or clothes or medicine.

For the next four years he remained with Mrs. Clemm

and her daughter Virginia in Baltimore, doing occasional writing and working in the library. He is described at this time as handsome and romantic-looking and popular, as always, with women.

In 1833, while still in Baltimore, he started to write short stories and literary criticism. His first real success was the winning of a prize of $50.00 offered by a weekly newspaper, the *Baltimore Sunday Visitor*, for his story "MS. Found in a Bottle". Though he was only twenty-four at the time, writers and publishers began to notice him. Had it not been for his constant bad health and his gradually increasing spells of drinking, his life might have been from that time on a comfortable one. Each time work worthy of him and security were within his grasp, however, his nerves would weaken and he would be "sick" again and unable to cope with the world, opium finally relieving him when drink failed. Of course, had it not been for his weaknesses, we might not have the remarkably original and brilliant tales which you have read.

His cousin, Virginia, was now growing up. His aunt wanted Poe to marry her when she was barely fourteen and he twenty-seven. To Mrs. Clemm it meant that the little family would always be together. To Poe it meant the security of a home and a family. Still, because of her youth and their blood relationship, he hesitated almost a year, only giving in when the loneliness of his life back in Richmond, where he had secured a position as editor of the *Southern Literary Messenger*, was too much for him. He and Virginia were married May 16, 1836, in Richmond, where she and Mrs. Clemm had come to make a home for him and to eke out an income with boarders and sewing.

VIRGINIA, CHILD-WIFE OF HER COUSIN, EDGAR ALLAN POE, AND INSPIRATION OF HIS BEAUTIFUL POEM, "ANNABEL LEE"

Much has been written about Poe's tenderness and devotion to his girl-wife. His love for her as a woman could not have been very strong at the time of their marriage. It grew with years, and she adored him. Very shortly after their marriage she developed tuberculosis and until her death ten years later was in constantly failing health. Poe lived in terror of her death, his mind constantly occupied with thoughts of it and fears that it would happen. You can see why he would write a story like "Ligeia" and one like "The Fall of the House of Usher," in which Roderick was himself and the Lady Madeline, Virginia. His own health weakened with hers. Spells of her sickness would be followed by drinking or drugs and then a prolonged illness of his own. He lived barely three years after her death. To her he wrote his beautiful poem, "Annabel Lee."

Once launched on an editorial career in Richmond in 1836, he spent the rest of his life at this sort of work, living also in Philadelphia, where he was editor of *Burton's Magazine* and *Graham's Magazine*, and in New York City, where he worked on the *Broadway Journal*. For all of these he wrote the finest literary criticism known in America up to this time. He published in these magazines the tales you have read in this book, winning a prize of $100.00 in Philadelphia for "The Gold Bug." At times he worked with boundless energy. In one year, for example, he published eighty-three reviews, four essays, six poems, and three stories. While he was working on it, he increased the circulation of *The Southern Literary Messenger* from 500 to 3,500 and of *Graham's Magazine* from 5,000 to 40,000. He corresponded with the famous American poet, James Russell Lowell. He met Washington Irving, William Cullen Bryant, and Dickens, who had come to this country on a lecture tour. He made plans to start his own literary magazine, which would be of national importance.

Through all the story runs the record of his drinking, his bad health, his poverty. He was never paid well for anything he did. Other writers earned their livings by teaching school or holding political posts. Poe had nothing but his writing to depend on. There were brief spells of prosperity. When he was living on Brandywine Street in Philadelphia, Virginia had a harp on which her husband taught her to play, and Mrs. Clemm had a beautiful red carpet! These periods were brief. Virginia would be sick or Poe would drink again and lose his position. Then the family would move, and Mrs. Clemm would have to manage on almost nothing.

The years spent in Philadelphia were probably the happiest in Poe's life. The little six-room house, with its garden, stood in what was then a lovely suburban section, outside the city proper, known as Spring Garden. This house has been purchased and restored by a group of Philadelphians. It is furnished as nearly as possible as records show it to have been furnished when Poe lived there. Here he wrote "The Raven" and many other poems and stories that rank among his best works, including several that you have read in this book. The house today is shabby and its furnishings as meagre as of old; the streets that surround it are closely built, bordered with warehouses, and noisy with traffic; but the pages that were written there shine brightly.

Poe's last home was a little workman's cottage in Fordham, now part of New York City, then nine miles out in the country. Here he brought Mrs. Clemm and Virginia in May, 1846. Before that they had been living in New

York City for almost two years, and Poe during this time had written his best poetry. "The Raven", published in 1845, had made him famous at once both here and in England. It was quoted everywhere. Poe received ten dollars for it. By then he was known as a remarkable person. He was welcome in a literary set which included famous women poets of the day. But the excitement of his success, the total illness of Virginia, and his own drinking had re-

EDGAR ALLAN POE COTTAGE IN POE PARK, BRONX, NEW YORK

duced him almost to insanity. In October, 1845, he collapsed completely and was forced to give up his editorship of the *Broadway Journal*, and with it his entire income. The Fordham cottage was humble but beautiful. It would have been comfortable had the family ever had enough food or fuel. A friend who visited in the winter of 1846 found Virginia sick in bed with only Poe's coat and the family cat to keep her warm. A collection was taken among Poe's friends after that; so Virginia was comfortable until she died, January 30, 1847. Poe was terribly sick at the time and might not have lived had it not been for Mrs. Clemm.

For the short time that still remained of his life after Virginia's death, Poe continued to devote himself to writing and to lecturing. But attacks of brain fever left him unable to work at all for long periods of time. Mrs. Clemm wanted him to marry again. She felt he needed some one in Virginia's place. There were numerous women in his life, too. The glamour he had always possessed had not lessened with the years. He became engaged to a poetess, Mrs. Sarah Helen Whitman of Providence, Rhode Island, but because of gossip about his irregular habits she refused at the last minute to marry him. He felt deep love for Mrs. Annie Richmond, of Lowell, Massachusetts, a married woman of strong and wonderful character who tried to help him. At one time, in despair over his future, he tried to commit suicide. Finally he turned from women to his writing again.

The last two months of his life he spent back in Richmond, Virginia. He left Mrs. Clemm with friends in Brooklyn, New York, saying to her at parting, "God bless you, my own darling mother. Don't fear for Eddie. See how good I will be while I am away from you, and will come back to love and comfort you." She never saw him again.

His life in Richmond for the short time he was there was peaceful and happy. He had always loved the place and was received in it now as a famous writer. He visited old friends and saw his sister Rosalie. He joined a society called "The Friends of Temperance" and hoped that through their influence he could give up drinking. He lectured and read "The Raven" to admiring audiences. And he was reunited with the sweetheart of his early days, Sarah Elmira Royster, who was a widow now, and to whom he became engaged a short time after their meeting. It was a strange match. To Poe it must have meant only security and comfort. There seemed to be little sentiment on either side, though he wrote Mrs. Clemm, "I think she loves me more devotedly than anyone I ever knew, and I cannot help loving her in return."

He started north on September 29, 1849, to close the cottage in Fordham and bring Mrs. Clemm back for the wedding. The night before he had given a lecture in Richmond and had attended a party with friends, taking the boat for Baltimore at four o'clock in the morning. He was quite possibly on the verge of a physical collapse when he left. For five days after his arrival in Baltimore he disappeared. Finally he was found unconscious and taken to a hospital, where he died after five days of alternate delirium and consciousness. His last words were, "Lord help my poor soul."

There are several explanations of his death. His mind may have given way entirely when he reached Baltimore. He may have yielded to his constant urge for drink. Or he may have been drugged by crooked politicians who were conducting an election in the city and seizing all strangers who might be forced to vote. No one will ever know just what happened. At the last a Baltimore cousin arranged for his comfort. He was buried in the churchyard of the Westminster Presbyterian Church, October 8, 1849. The search for Eldorado, unsuccessful, tragic, was ended.

In the Metropolitan Museum of Art in New York City, the actors' memorial to him says, "He was great in his genius; unhappy in his life; wretched in his death; but in his fame he is immortal."

POE'S LAST RESTING PLACE, BALTIMORE, MARYLAND

# THOUGHTS AND QUERIES

## I. GENERAL

1. Most modern detective stories follow the same plot pattern. A crime is committed. There seem to be no clues for its solution. The clever detective, however, uncovers all the evidence. After he has solved the problem, he explains the steps which he has followed. Poe, who invented this type of story, uses this method. Show how he does this in two of these tales.
2. Compare Dupin in character and in method with Charlie Chan or Ellery Queen or with any other "master mind" you know.
3. "Pseudo-scientific" stories are popular today. Poe makes his, like "A Descent into the Maelström" or "MS. Found in a Bottle", seem actually possible. How does he accomplish this? Does "Superman" impress you in the same way? What about some of the other wonder stories you have read?
4. Do you think it is necessary for characters in stories like these to seem like real people? In which of Poe's tales do the characters seem real?
5. What experiences of the author gave him material for these stories? How does his life account for the gloom in a great many of them?
6. Poe's favorite stories were Ligeia, The Gold Bug, The Murders in the Rue Morgue, The Fall of the House of Usher, The Tell-Tale Heart, The Black Cat, William

Wilson, and A Descent into the Maelström. What are yours? If you differ from Poe, can you account for the difference?

## II. SPECIFIC

### *The Gold Bug*

1. In Poe's day there was a great interest in cryptograms. In 1840, when the author was working for *Graham's Magazine*, he challenged anyone to send him a cipher which he couldn't solve. For a time he published all of those sent in, with his solution of them.

   Were you interested in the code in this story? Did you understand how Legrand started to figure it out? See if you can make up a very simple code of your own for the class to solve.
2. Do you know any other stories of buried treasure? Try writing one.
3. Look up Captain Kidd for a class report. Invent a story with him as the hero.

### *The Murders in the Rue Morgue*

1. Compare Dupin with Sherlock Holmes as a man and as a detective.
2. This story was translated into French as soon as it was published and has always been immensely popular in France. Would it seem as interesting if it had taken place in New York or Chicago? Does the setting of it add to the mystery and the horror?
3. What details does Poe put in which make this seem like an account of an actual happening?

*The Purloined Letter*

1. Pretend you are the Minister from whom Dupin recovered the letter. Tell what happened when he discovered it was gone.
2. Tell the story from the viewpoint of the lady from whom it was stolen.
3. Do you agree with what the author has to say about poets and mathematicians?
4. Why does he exaggerate the care with which the Paris police searched for the letter?

*The Tell-Tale Heart*

1. This story can often be heard on the radio. On which programs would it be most appropriate?
2. Choose some student in the class who is good at dramatics and have him read the story aloud.
3. How does the author succeed in keeping you in suspense? Which part seemed most dramatic to you, the murder or the confession?

*The Black Cat*

1. This story was made into a moving picture several years ago. Which scenes in it would be most exciting?
2. Show how the character of the murderer grew steadily worse under the influence of drink.

*The Cask of Amontillado*

1. Why was it effective to have the victim masquerading as a clown?
2. How did the murderer succeed in getting his victim exactly where he wanted him?

3. Why is Rome an appropriate setting for this story?
4. Look up Carnivals in Rome and give a class report on them.

*Ligeia*

1. Why is the heroine's strong will emphasized at the beginning of the story?
2. Poe often described extravagantly beautiful and luxurious homes like the one in this story. Explain this from what you know about his life.

*The Fall of the House of Usher*

1. Have you ever witnessed a tornado or a hurricane? If so, compare it with the storm described in this story.
2. Write a character sketch of Roderick. Remember Poe was describing himself in this character.
3. What purpose does the reading aloud serve?
4. Can you see why *The Haunted Castle* should be considered one of the finest American poems?

*MS. Found in a Bottle*

1. Does Poe mean you to take this story seriously?
2. Look up the story of the "Flying Dutchman" and compare it with this.
3. Make up a story of your own about a manuscript found in a bottle.

*The Masque of the Red Death*

1. Poe was not especially interested in teaching lessons. This story, however, seems to "moralize". What can you learn from it?

2. Were you prepared for the plague to get into the castle in some way? Discuss this point.

*A Descent into the Maelström*

1. What incident in the "Odyssey" may have given Poe an idea for this story?
2. Why would the happenings of this story be impossible?
3. How does the author make them seem convincing?

*William Wilson*

1. To what extent is Poe himself William Wilson?
2. What is an allegory? Could you class this story as one?
3. List the hints which Poe gives you that the second William Wilson is not a real person. What happened after he was murdered?

*The Pit and the Pendulum*

1. The Inquisition features in the novel, "Captain from Castile," by Samuel Shellabarger. Perhaps someone in the class would read the book and make a report on it. How does the author compare Naziism and the Inquisition?
2. Rats seem to be popular in stories. What others do you know that involve them?
3. Does Poe's ending seem abrupt to you? Should he have hinted earlier in the story that the victim would escape?

UNIV. of VIRGINIA

RICHMOND

THE ALLANS

SULLIVAN'S ISLAND

ARMY POST —

SETTING OF GOLD BUG

Atlantic

N

POE'S TRAVELS